THE LOST CHAPTER

THE GRIMM STAR UNIVERSE

J. DARLENE EVERLY

J. DARLENE EVERLY

THE LOST CHAPTER

The Grimm Star Universe

Hardcover: ISBN 978-1-954719-02-6
Paperback: ISBN 978-1-954719-01-9
Ebook: ISBN 978-1-954719-00-2
First paperback edition February 2021.
Edited by Beth Hale, Magnolia Editing.
Cover art by Jupiter Alley.
Layout by Beth Hale, Magnolia Editing.

✽ Created with Vellum

DEDICATION

This book is dedicated to the purple haired waitress who gave a writer in need a pen.

1

ARIELLA WANTED TO GET AS FAR AWAY AS POSSIBLE. EVERYONE
else had choices; everyone else was free to decide for themselves. But, of course, she would be the only one subject to the
ritual, and every day it got closer was one less day when she was
able to go on pretending to not hate her station.

She swam into the current of the heat vent where she slept
and curled up. For now, she didn't have to go to the palace, not
for another two weeks. For now, she could just be and enjoy her
small part of the water.

"Hey, are you going to come with me or not?" Miranda
asked, swimming on the just the other side of the vent.

Part of her wanted to say yes, she was going to go back on
her word and stay behind to sleep and hide until her whole life
changed. But the thing she liked best in the world was going on
scavenger trips with her friend. And if she only had two weeks
left of her own life, she should spend it doing her favorite
things, especially things like scavenging that would never be
allowed after the ritual.

With a sigh, Ariella swam out of the vent and past her friend.

Miranda whooped and darted after her.

"As long as we can avoid running into-" Ariella swallowed the rest of her words because the last person she wanted to see was heading their way.

"Crab shit," Miranda cursed next to her.

"Yep. He has a damn radar or something." Ariella scowled at Fantos, the handsome but cruel vessel of the gods as he wandered their way, his face clouded and his eyes focused through the arches to the main area beyond.

"Let's go around." Miranda shoved Ariella out one of the large arches and into the league long courtyard in the center of the walled areas.

"Is there some way we can make him go to the surface," Ariella said, her voice a growl, but she winked at Miranda and finished by saying, "and leave him up there forever?"

"Please, yes." Miranda laughed as they swam up and beyond the confines of their usual world.

"What I want to know is, why did the gods choose him?" Miranda shook her head, the water around them darkened as they went beyond the range of the coral lights of the city and into the cold, black part of the water.

And why did the gods choose me, Ariella wanted to add. But she never said it out loud, she never allowed herself the release of putting the vibrations out into the water for fear someone would pick them up.

"Some of the people at the sanctuary believe his choosing is a bad sign, that it means threat and war are coming. It may be the best explanation for why he was chosen so late; King Ellias died tides and tides ago." Ariella increased her speed because talking about the theories of looming disaster that were floating so thick in the sanctuary, among her brethren, made her nervous and feel like outrunning them was the only thing she should be worried about.

Miranda put a shaking hand on Ariella's arm, anchoring them together as they swam through the dark.

"But who would declare war on the sanctuary?" Miranda's voice was hushed and her vibration through the water was heavy with fear and imagined pain.

"No one knows, and it kind of makes no sense." The water around them started to turn light again, their passage through the deep ending as they grew ever closer to the surface.

"So," Ariella said, shaking her head and smiling a tremulous smile, "what are we looking for today?"

"If the gods are with us, we'll find the star trillium herb. It has three little petals that loop around on itself to form a sort of orb with pieces missing that you can see the stem through," Miranda said, trying, and failing, to form the shape with her fingers.

"Like this?" Ariella flicked her hand and held a swirling ball of water in her other as it moved into what she thought the shape of the plant was.

Miranda grabbed Ariella's hovering hand and poked the orb with Ariella's fingers to correct the shape.

"Close, but more like this."

"Oh, I think I've seen this before," Ariella said, dropping the orb so that it morphed back into just water.

"Where? Because we looked yesterday too and couldn't find it. The sanctuary needs it, they're almost out, and I'm afraid that if I don't find it I'll get stuck in the store room for a month." Miranda scrunched up her nose and Ariella laughed.

"It was on the big island in a big patch by the copse of tall trees; do you know where I'm talking about?"

"The same island we found the thorn flower on?"

"Yes, near the same spot." Ariella dodged around a lumbering transporter as it headed to the surface to be filled with whatever they found that Miranda thought the sanctuary or other supply storage needed.

"Do we have to morph?" Miranda grimaced and hugged her arms into her chest.

Ariella didn't like the process either, but she couldn't very well tell Miranda that. Miranda didn't have magic that made it less painful. Ariella's magic didn't stop the pain entirely, and the longer she was on land, walking and breathing air, the more painful it got, but for Miranda, there wasn't even the delay in full nerve onslaught.

"I'll morph; you can check the perimeter of the island, and if I find the plant, you can morph to help collect enough so we can be done faster," Ariella said and Miranda let her arms float free while a small smile formed on her face and her blue hair flowed behind her.

The last consort mother had blue hair so for some reason Ariella always assumed Miranda or one of the other blue haired girls would develop magic and be marked for consort mother.

Instead, her red hair burst into flames a year before Fantos developed powers.

Now, she waited for the auspicious tide the sanctuary predicted for her marriage to a man she hated, all because the gods had a cruel streak and crab shit sense of humor.

But first, she was going to walk around on the island, help Miranda, and pretend it wasn't happening for a few hours.

2

———————————

Most of the islands around were too small for anyone to get lost on, most of the islands were so small you could see across them to the other side.

Sometimes they were hard to find because they would float with the tide to wherever it took them, and occasionally they disappeared entirely, swamped beneath the waves and taken apart by the water. But the plants kept trying, the floating flotsam and jetsam kept reforming little islands, and the big island was the oldest and by far the largest of any they knew of.

Which made it easier to find, and more painful to do the search of.

"Okay, I feel the vibrations directly ahead. How about you?" Miranda asked.

Ariella tried not to roll her eyes. Ever since her powers manifested, Miranda doubted her own most basic skills.

"You already know you're right." Her sense of vibration had not changed, and neither had her magic included any better way to sense direction and the movement of things in the water. The weird self-doubt she inspired in people just by being the recipient of the gods terrible idea frustrated her.

They neared the island a wave of force knocked them off their course, sending them both tumbling end over end like they were hit by a rogue force pressure from Fantos.

"What was that?" Ariella asked, shaking out her tail and catching up to Miranda, they both turned their gazes to the island, it's dark underside above them.

"No idea, but we should be careful." Miranda started swimming toward the island again and turned her head to ask over her shoulder, "Are you sure Fantos wasn't coming up here today for something?"

"He doesn't leave the grounds other than to go to the training trench." Ariella made it her business to know about his whereabouts as much as possible. She hated running into him at all, let alone when she didn't expect it like the narrowly avoided encounter earlier.

"The gods only gift two people with powers at a time, right?" Miranda's eyes were wide and her mouth popped open and stayed that way as she looked ahead.

Ariella could practically hear the question waiting in Miranda's brain. Was there another person gifted by the gods, were their powers the same as Fantos's. It was a stupid question, one she had asked of the witch of the sanctuary herself when he was chosen. It was a hollow hope then, but she couldn't fault Miranda for having it.

"Only two are ever chosen. And few Kings in history have been given the war gifts. This must be something different." Ariella sped up, because maybe the thing that caused the force was something she could use to get her out of the ritual.

Miranda followed in her wake, falling silent and her face falling into grim lines.

From below, the island looked the same as it ever did, a

tangled mass of vegetation that trailed and waved in the water, this one's dragging branches thicker and going deeper into the water than the other, smaller islands roots.

The light around the island was tinged in the green glow of healthy plants that lined the outside of it, projecting their light even in the middle of the day. The green light was one of Ariella's favorite things about the surface. No green glow existed in the deep, just the pinks, yellows, and blues of the lights of the coral they so relied on.

Maybe someday this island would get deep enough that the plant could hit the sea floor and anchor itself there, she always hoped it would and that it would and when it did it would shine its green light into her world.

"Where should we go up? I don't remember which side is closer to the area where the plant is growing," Miranda said.

"Over by that new little branch is the quickest way to the plant, I think," Ariella said, pointing to one end of the island where new growth grew even more brightly than the rest of the edge of the island.

"Are you still sure you want to morph by yourself? After that force, I'm not sure it's such a good idea." Miranda put her hand on her arm and bit her lip.

"I'll be fine. Don't worry about me. Besides I'm sure it's just a natural thing we don't know about. We don't spend a whole lot of time up here. There could be a whole new animal that is birthing something and crabbed off about it." Ariella bumped Miranda's tail with her own while they both laughed.

"Well, I'll still go around the shoreline, and if you run into trouble, send me an orb." Miranda smiled and Ariella smiled back, imagining developing the ability to trap a message in an orb of water beyond just its existence.

She could form an orb of water from the vapor in the air

even, but manage to speak in air and not water, no the gods didn't see the need to grant her with that ability.

They neared the surface and waited, an inch below the water line while the scanned the small area of the shore they could see from their positions.

Nothing. The surface looked as it ever did, with no more sign of something to worry about than the waiting pain of the morph and possibly a hard search for the plant if Ariella's memory was faulty.

Miranda popped her head out of the water without a single splash and Ariella did the same, each of them as still as they could be while the water lapped the shore in front of them.

Ariella ducked her mouth below the water line and said, "I'll get back here with the plant as soon as I can."

Her friend nodded and Ariella grabbed onto the slimy edge of the island, using her tail to propel her out of the water and onto the vegetation.

She closed her eyes and focused her mind on her breathing and her ability to walk.

In her chest, her lungs screamed, crying in pain as they shifted to accepting air directly from the gases around her and not through the water.

While her tail tickled, then prickled, then wailed while it split itself and felt like it was turning inside out to shift into two legs, full of muscles that quavered and shook as she watched them become the same skin as her hands.

Pain seared through her lungs and her new legs were instantly exhausted, the unfamiliar muscles in them felt like a mass of bruises, but she put a hand to one and then the other flowing water back into the tissue in such a way that she was wavier than a second before. Her legs looked like she was wearing the thinnest layer of water over them.

There was less she could do about the pain in her lungs. Her land lungs couldn't be given a layer of water or she would die.

So, she did the only thing she could; she took a deep, agonizing breath and got to her feet while the water flowed around them at a faster pace to keep the pain at a dull roar.

Ariella's first steps were always careful, they had to be. A fall when she was morphed sounded like one of the worst ideas she could imagine, she had never experienced one and she didn't intend to.

But she couldn't just focus on the steps and keeping the pain at bay; she had a job to do and she had to keep an eye out for anything dangerous, so the pain leaked in at the edges more than it usually would.

The strange smells, stronger for being in the air and crushed under her feet, always made her head ache, but they were worse than normal and a spearing sensation started just behind her left eye.

"Great," she mumbled to herself, the sound not coming out at all since her vocal cords weren't coated with water. "Just get to the plants and get off the damn island."

Moving through the foliage, carefully placing each foot before she put her weight on it so her legs could get accustomed, only made it more frustrating when all she wanted was to go faster.

The bog area of the island was on the interior and surrounded by a ring of tall trees that swayed in the breeze, their longs limbs and fronds like the feathers of the birds that flew through them.

Getting closer, something visible through the trees caught her eye and she crouched down to more easily blend into the bushes she navigated around.

Something glinted in the sun, the shine coming off of it

reaching from the ground to as far upward through the branches that she could make out.

What was that? It wasn't there the last time she came to the island, and as far as she knew no one brought anything to the island, they just used it for collecting things they could use. And there were no plants or surface animals she was aware of that shined in such a way or were as large.

Certainly no bird could have built such a large nest, but she could think of little else that would be responsible as she crept forward, wary of one of the only things she had ever encountered that was completely bizarre.

She stopped at the edge of the trees and tried to make sense of what she was seeing, tried to name the thing in front of her. She didn't have the words.

3

RIGHT IN THE MIDDLE OF THE BOG SAT A LARGE SHINY OBJECT, cylindrical and smaller at the bottom than it seemed at the top, it didn't move or make any noise.

Just to the left of her spot in the trees a panel opened on the lower side of the object, lowering to the ground.

People walked out, but they wore some kind of wrap that hugged their bodies in a single piece, so different from the wraps her people wore she didn't understand how they moved in them.

The people all had varying skin colors, which wasn't surprising to her, but unlike her own people, these people's hair was all versions of brown, some so light it looked yellow, some so dark it looked black, but still shades on the same spectrum and some of them had baby short hair although they looked fully grown, all the others kept their hair trapped by some magic so it stayed away from their face.

Her people's hair was all vibrant colors and she grabbed a dripping lock of her own red hair to stare at it before she looked back at these strange people and cocked her head to the side.

One of the people held a circle in front of them and poked away at the nothing in the center of it like they were actually doing something. The other people were touching things and speaking to each other, their voices muffled by the wind in the leaves all around her. She used some water to flow into her ears to make it easier to understand, among her own people were different languages. Not that anyone was aware when the water was interpreting, but they knew when anyone etched an eel skin scroll that all along they were speaking different languages.

She wanted to get closer, but who were these people? And why didn't she know them?

Grey, the color of their wraps blocked her view of the others for a minute and she tilted her head back to see the whole of the person standing with their back to her. The person was tall, but they had the baby short hair, like it was just growing in and… their legs.

Leaning from side to side to check, and then peering around their body, she double checked all the other people she could see.

None of them had water pouring around their legs, so they couldn't have magic, but they didn't do the odd half step, half jerk gait her people did when they were morphed. These people moved more gracefully on land than even she did shielded by her magic.

What did that mean?

Ariella couldn't make sense out of any of it, and she didn't trust the strangers enough to continue on into the bog and risk running into them.

She slunk through the small bushes, hoping to find at least a couple plants to bring back to Miranda because she was sure no one but Fantos and the protectorate would be allowed to come up here until the strangers were dealt with.

Miranda said the sanctuary needed the plants, so Ariella would get as many as she could before she had to get away from these people.

Just around a bush she spotted a few of the plants in between two trees, the space wider and wetter between those two trees than between the others she had passed.

Her legs screamed at her as she kneeled down and pulled a few from the ground, putting them to her side where her water grabbed them and held them for her, letting her hands remain free to grab some more.

If she took all of these, at least the very reason for the trip wouldn't be lost.

Besides, it gave her more time to watch the strange people.

Footsteps, the sound of squelching ground, sounded on the other side of the trees close to where she kneeled down.

She froze. Her hand hovering over one of the plants she intended to pull, the only thing she allowed to move was her chest as it filled and emptied with shallow breaths and the water flowing around her and holding onto the plants she already collected.

The person who came into view on the other side of the tree was one of the baby haired ones. His hair was almost black and stuck up from his head in wild curls while he skin was a medium brown color like Miranda's.

"It's going to take a lot more terraforming than I was hoping," the person said, speaking to someone Ariella realized was standing on the other side of the tree from her that she couldn't see. The person's voice was low and deep and he sat down on a large shell half smothering a small bush.

"Evik, we knew it was mostly a water covered planet." The person on the other side of the tree also had a deep voice and it sounded like they found the whole thing amusing. Not that

Ariella could figure out what any of it meant, although she thought Evik was the sitting person's name.

Maybe someone at the sanctuary would know what they meant. She thought listening and bringing back as much information as she could was the best thing, but her knees were killing her and she was going to have to move soon her muscles told her.

"Yeah, but Temple and the rest of the ship won't be able to come down for a while. How long do you think it will take?" Evik asked, leaning forward to rest his elbows on his knees.

Her knees sent a fresh wave of pain racing through her in sympathy. Who leaned on their legs like that? What were these people and their strange powers?

"I have no idea. We just figure it out, that's all. We'll see them all soon enough. Don't worry, dude." A hand clapped Evik on the shoulder, making Ariella jump and freeze again, taking tiny breaths to stop them from discovering her.

Stupid idea to go after the damn plants, she thought.

"Keep moving forward, right?" Evik asked, his mouth screwed up to one side and his voice sending out the vibration that whatever they were talking about he thought it was irritating at best. Dude was the name for the male species of sea slug they ate. So this Evik had to be a he.

"Always," the person said, their vibration taking on a harsh note. "Listen," their voice softened so she had to strain to hear it, and gone was the hard edge to their vibration. "I know it's hardest right after a tragedy. But the sooner you embrace it, the easier it will be to move on."

Evik nodded once. The gesture was perfunctory and his face still looked troubled. A line formed between his brows and he dropped his eyes to the ground in front of him while the squelching sound of the person on the other side of the tree let Ariella know they had moved off to further in the bog.

Whatever his tragedy had been, Ariella thought telling him to just move on wasn't going to work, and was just plain cruel.

A pang of sympathy went through her and made her sad on his behalf. That he would have a tragedy, no matter how strange he was, was bad enough. But the lack of understanding from what seemed to be his friend, and was definitely one of his own people, reminded her of the witch and Fantos. Two of her least favorite people and reason enough to worry about sounding the alarm about the strangers's presence.

He stood up and brushed off the back of his wrap where he was sitting on it before he walked away too.

She took a deep breath and finally dropped her hand from where it had hung in the air.

Deep in her shoulder, a tiny muscle ached from holding her arm aloft for so long, but she pulled the remaining plants before her and placed them at her side in the water with the others.

Maybe she could use her position, her powers, to convince the protectorate and Fantos to let these people go back to wherever they came from. Maybe she could avoid a more violent response from Fantos, which seemed to be his most common response to anything.

Ariella got back to her crouched position, pulling more water to her to ease some of the ache setting into her legs, and moved back through the bushes the way she had come. Going to the shore as fast as she could without drawing attention to herself was not as fast as she wanted, again.

Nothing of the day was happening the way she hoped.

She probably should have stayed in her vent, she thought, allowing herself a grim smile.

The shore came into view and she breathed deeper, the sound of the water calling to her and calming her mind that roiled with thoughts of the strangers and what would happen when she reported their presence.

Before she could step back into the water, while scales started to pop out of the skin of her legs and the agony of morphing was ripping through her again, a force threw her off her feet and from the island, sending her flying through the air before she crashed into the waves.

4

THE FIRST TIME FANTOS MANIFESTED HIS POWERS SHE WAS unfortunate enough to be near him. The force if it was enough to send her toppling through the water in the courtyard to slam into one of the arches.

Hitting the water at the speed she was going and the angle her body was flying through the air felt the same.

All at once she was in the water and her morph was complete, her legs replaced by her tail and every scale of it ached so it floated lifeless in the water.

The plants she had risked discovery for bobbed on the water above her head.

She forced her weary tail to move enough that she was propelled upward, grabbing the plants, counting to make sure she got them all.

Expending that much effort left her oddly exhausted, and clutching the plants to her chest she yelled Miranda's name into the water and that she was dropping.

It didn't take long for Miranda to make it to her, her blue

hair flying out behind her and her face wearing the same shock Ariella felt in her bones.

"Did you feel that? It felt like a force pressure again. But that's impossible," Miranda said in rapid fire as she came to Ariella and took the plants from her hands to put them in a net she kept at her side.

"Yes, but it got me while I was on the island," Ariella said, letting the water drag her down instead of using her tail.

"Oh my gods, are you hurt?" Miranda took her gently but the elbow and swam for both of them.

"Nothing bad, just really," Ariella said, pausing to yawn, "really sore and tired."

The water in front of her blinked to black, not the gradual darkening as they went deeper, just black like she had shut her eyes, but she was sure they were still open.

She was still awake enough to know that Miranda was calling her name and asking her to wake up, but that faded too until she was alone in the vast sea of her world feeling no vibrations, hearing no words, and devoid of sensation from her body. Until she was nothing at all.

Coming to, Ariella first became aware of Miranda's hand on her arm and next of the speed they were traveling.

Next came the darkness of the depth they were at and the chill of the water.

"Slow down," she got out of a still half closed throat.

"Ariella." Miranda's vibration was all relief and shock, but she slowed and her grip on Ariella's arm loosened.

"What happened?" Miranda's voice was hushed and there was fear laced in words.

"I don't know, but I think it was that force that hit me in the air. It's definitely worse on the surface. I don't know how those people withstand it.

"People?"

Ariella squeezed her eyes shut, trying to find the words to explain what she had seen that wouldn't scare the crab shit out of her friend. But her brain was still only half working and shivers moved up and down her body.

"I promise I will explain, but I need to get to my vent and sleep before I can make sense of it enough to speak." Like it was trying to prove her point, her vision blinked out and she knew she was going to pass out again.

"But," Miranda started and groaned when Ariella went limp again. "Crab shit."

Unlike last time, Ariella was blinking in and out as they went through the water to the back way into her chambers, her body shivered violently by the time Miranda swam her into her vent and the heat began to seep into her bones.

Finally, oh finally, Ariella gave up the fight to stay awake and closed her eyes to sleep, the strange people, words, and shining object floating through her mind.

5

Blinking her eyes, Ariella had a moment where she forgot the island and everything she saw there.

When it came back to her like a wave, washing through her with knowledge and fresh concern, she sat up in her vent.

"Oh, thank the gods, you're awake," Miranda said, popping into her vent and curling her tail under her so she was floating right next to Ariella.

"So… what happened?" Miranda's eyebrows shot up and she bit her lip, her vibration trepidatious as well as curious.

Ariella shuddered and curled tighter in upon herself. How was she going to answer the question of what happened when she didn't really understand it herself.

"I don't know what caused that force, or why it hit me harder when I was on the surface and not in the water."

Miranda sucked in her bottom lip and furrowed her brow, it didn't surprise Ariella that her friend was confused. She hadn't actually answered a damn thing. Yet.

"There are people on the island." Ariella's voice was hushed and the skin of her arms tingled saying it out loud.

"Who was up there? I thought we were the only ones the sanctuary sent," Miranda said, she didn't look concerned anymore, she looked pissed.

"Not our people, other people were up there. They had a huge strange curved wall with them and they were walking around like it didn't hurt them." Ariella shook her head, her eyes wide. "I've never seen anything like it."

"You need to tell the sanctuary." Miranda's face looked ashen, her eyes were wide, and her mouth stayed hanging open after she was done speaking.

"I know, but it doesn't make any sense. I want to go find out what they're doing up there first. Maybe they're from another sea we don't know about and they can help up when we go to the surface. Maybe they found the answer to the pain of morphing." Ariella reached out a hand and tried to touch Miranda's arm, but stopped short as Miranda grew rigid.

"Ari, we need to tell them right now. Those people might be why Fantos was given the war gifts after so long without them." The how do you not realize that riding in her tone was not lost on Ariella.

"Trust me, Mir. Please. I don't want to risk Fantos losing his control on people who may be innocent. And they may even be a victim of whatever that force was that I got hit with. I need to find out if they should be sent on their way or brought before the witch, or if I should notify the whole sanctuary and let them tell Fantos. I can't just know what the right thing to do is. Clairvoyance was not one of my gifts." Ariella tried for a shaky smile at her not funny, nor well timed joke, but it broke through Miranda's walls and she gave her a tremulous smile back.

"I'm only going to agree to this if you let me come with you and keep an eye on you, you know that, right?" She looked like she might vomit just thinking about it, but it helped settle Ariella's nerves.

"Nothing would be better than to know you're in the water waiting to intervene if I need you too." Ariella thought she may as well lay the groundwork for their excursion. The last thing she wanted was to bring Miranda with her and put her at risk by asking her to morph. No, she was going to take the biggest risk by herself. She also wanted to find out and decide for herself since she was the only one who was going to be able to understand their language in the air. And after Miranda's talk of going to the sanctuary right away, Ariella wasn't sure she trusted her friend to wait long enough to understand.

"But Ari, are you sure you're up to this? You don't look so great right now."

"Yes. I'm sure. I can do this, but I need an hour or two more here and something to eat before I do it all again." What she really wanted was a week more to sleep too much before she had to go back up. But not only were they risking someone else going to the surface and making the discovery before they figured it all out, she didn't have a lot of time before the ritual.

She didn't have a lot of time, period.

Miranda tapped her on the arm and swam away, while Ariella relaxed back into her vent, allowing herself to drop closer to the very place it came out of the ground so she could get even more warmth from it and hoped it would make her muscles relax.

Whatever that force was, every part of her hurt.

She ran a hand along her tail and a few of the scales sloughed off and floated around her.

A hard lump formed in her stomach, going back to the surface was a huge risk. What had it done to her?

How had her gifts not protected her? Of course the water gave Miranda protection, but her gifts should have done the same for Ariella.

Thoughts raced around her mind faster than a rogue wave. What did it mean?

Doubt flooded through her and her hands shook as she raised them and shoved them to the other side of the vent current where the chill of the outside water felt icier than usual.

She pushed and an orb formed in front of her to shoot to the opposite wall a second later shaking the room with its force.

Breathing in a heavy breath of relief and slumping back down to curl in upon herself again, Ariella wasn't sure what it was about the force she was hit with or the scales she lost that made her doubt her magic. She knew better.

Maybe she had not wanted the magic, and maybe she cursed it more than once after Fantos was gifted too, but to doubt its very presence in her, to think that some unknown thing could cause the gifts of the gods themselves to be stripped from her, that was just foolish.

In no sea, could she tell Miranda or anyone else that a doubt had ever entered her mind. The sanctuary would never let that kind of story spread. The ritual would be moved up the timeline. And she wanted more than anything to have it not happen at all.

The best she could hope for would be to talk to these people, find out what they were doing, what the force was if they knew, and send them back to wherever they came from.

No good would possibly come of Fantos or the sanctuary and the witch finding out. She had no doubt about that at all.

6

———————

Miranda kept closer to Ariella's side than she had on their first assent. Ariella tried not to get frustrated when their tails bumped again. She just tried to match her friend's rhythm so it would stop happening.

Neither of them carried a collecting net with them, but Ariella wondered if they should have, if for no other reason than to give them a likely story on their return.

The chances of someone seeing them, looking for them, or even intercepting their mission were high no matter what subterfuge Miranda had worked while Ariella tried to regain her strength.

She shook her head and tried to focus. At some point she was going to have to come up with what she was going to say.

The hour she spent in her vent had not proved helpful in the idea forming department, nor had the swim through the dark, but with the island looming above them, she was running out of time to come up with something.

Miranda grabbed hold of her arm and they stopped in place, suspended in the water around them.

"What's wrong?"

"Ari, I don't know if we should really be doing this. Maybe we should turn around. I mean," Miranda said, letting her voice trail off and hang there beside them, the weight of her concern riding in the current. "What if the force hits you again?"

There was no good answer to that so she swallowed and looked back up at the bottom of the island, no sunlight peeking around the edge this time of night to make the edges distinct, it was more of a shadow, a darker black, than the rest of the world.

"If it hits me again, I'm going to be fine. I have my magic with me, the gods are protecting me." She turned back to her friend and tried to paint her face in more belief than she actually had in her own statement.

"Okay, but don't do anything to get yourself hurt. If these people threaten you at all, get back in the damn water. Don't even wait to morph. Just get in the water right away. It's safer down here," Miranda said, starting to swim again.

Safer down here… Don't wait to morph… Ariella rushed to catch up with her friend, but her brain was stuck on the idea that it was safer in the water. Because it was. She knew that. But it had not occurred to her that the answer to why the force hit her so hard on the surface was because it hit her when she had dropped her veil of water but before she could morph fully back to herself, it got her when she was her most vulnerable.

It made it easier for her to keep moving, to set aside her fear and doubt. This time, she wasn't going to drop her veil and morph in the air.

As always, the water, and the gods that ruled it, were offering her what she needed and protecting her.

Miranda reached the surface first, only popping enough of her head above the water to see further into the interior of the island.

Everything was dark and quiet, there was no sign, as there had not been any when they were there last, of the people.

But… something was different.

While Miranda was rigid beside her, with her brow furrowed and her gaze darting around, Ariella knew the second she saw the island herself that it was larger, and very, very different.

The plants that made up the island grew at a steady rate, but somehow the shore of the island had expanded measurably. No longer a narrow band of mostly half formed plants and detritus, the shore was now thick and deep. It looked like it was the wrong color, like it was brown, but she wasn't sure in the dark if that was just the shadows of the trees that towered over everything.

On the islands all over the planet, the trees were usually no higher than two of her, but these trees would have measured many Fantos stacked up.

"Don't like that," Miranda muttered. "What in the water did this?"

"Nothing," Ariella said. "Nothing in the water did this. This is something entirely different."

She bit her lip and took a deep breath. It only made sense that the people on the island had something to do with it, but she couldn't imagine how that would be. Unless they were gifted too.

Gifts in the bodies of these strange people set her teeth on edge, sure she thought maybe they had them because they walked around so easily, but plant gifts? She had never heard of such a thing. And she didn't know what it meant.

Focusing was hard, but she managed and the morph rippled through her carrying agony with it.

"What are you doing?" Miranda cried, grabbing onto her

arm and shoving her face further out of the water as she started to sink while the pain rendered her unable to move.

"Ow," Ariella said, shaking her head and moving her legs around, the water a cool balm over the frayed nerves of them.

"Yeah, ow. That was stupid." Miranda's words were harsh, but her vibration only held fear and relief.

"Maybe, but now I can use my gift before I even step onto the shore, that should help protect me more." Ariella kicked and Miranda swam with her. Her friend remained stiff by her side, but she knew it was right decision when she stepped onto the shore and her veil was already in place.

She pulled more with her from the sea itself instead of from the air, using the water to fill her ears for interpreting their words, and cover her entire body from neck to feet and creating the illusion that she was wearing something similar to the grey thing the people wore.

If she was going to have a chance to get one of the them to talk to her and tell her what was going on up here, she thought it best if she looked as like them as possible.

Maybe her bright red hair would mark her as different, but there was less she could do about that. As it was, the veil around her was a poor approximation of the thing they wore and hers undulated constantly over her body.

Ariella bit her lip and hoped that whoever she talked to wouldn't notice in the darkness.

Darkness above the water was different than darkness under it. Brightness was too.

One of the guides at the sanctuary tried to explain to her once about what happened to their eyes on the surface, but it still didn't make any sense.

It didn't make sense, but it did make it harder to pick her way through the vegetation on the ground. Each step seemed to get her feet tangled in vines or risk her tripping over a branch.

But through the constant buzzing of the pain and the careful steps she was forced to take, she finally got to the edge of the clearing where the massive grey wall filled sat.

The people from earlier weren't milling about, but two sat around a small crackling ball of what looked like red magic.

So they did have magic.

Or maybe it was some kind of plant that she didn't know about. But if it was, it occasionally sent up seeds into the atmosphere.

Ariella leaned further into the clearing and realized one of the people sitting around the snapping red ball was asleep.

How did they stay morphed when they were asleep? She had to keep the thought of legs running at a low hum in the back of her mind the entire time she was on land, or she would start to morph back to her real form.

That was one of the basic tenants of being morphed and was part of the reason it hurt, how much magic did these people have that they could just sleep and walk around like their legs were fine and didn't hurt.

None of it made sense to Ariella, and while she chewed on her lip it made her want to talk to one of them sink beneath her roiling thoughts.

But she had to do it. She had to trust her own magic would protect her from theirs.

Trust.

She stepped into the clearing, the light from the red magic revealing her to the same man she saw by the tree.

His eyes widened and his mouth dropped open.

7

HE STUMBLED TO HIS FEET AND FOR THE FIRST TIME LOOKED LIKE one of her people when they had legs.

Maybe the magic of these people wasn't as strong as she thought.

It made her stand up straighter.

"Where did you come from? No other spindle was supposed to be sent down yet. How did you get to this island?" he asked, his voice was hushed and it had a strange timbre to it that scrambled her ability to fully grasp at the vibration it sent off.

She thought he was just surprised and confused, but she couldn't be sure there wasn't suspicion there too.

Her mouth opened and closed again. He wouldn't be able to understand her if she spoke in her language, she was sure of that.

At her side, she waved her fingers and hoped he didn't notice.

Water from the air collected in his ears and he shook his head, rubbing at one.

"I don't speak well," she said, trying for something that would invite him to continue the conversation on his side and stop asking questions.

"Sorry, my ears are bothering me all of the sudden," he said, walking away from the light and closer to her, which was great as far as she was concerned because the sleeping one didn't stir.

If things got out of hand, it would be easier to handle just one of them.

"Now, what did you say again?"

"My voice. It's having trouble." Maybe that would be a message that he would understand better.

"Oh," he said, his shoulders relaxing and small smile tugging at the corners of his mouth. "It's probably this place. The humidity is so thick it feels like walking through a blanket all the time. Wesson keeps getting headaches from it."

He made his way closer to her still and smiled at her, open and welcoming, like his surprise from before was forgotten. Strange, apparently just commenting on the climate was enough to distract this person into dropping his guard.

"Your face is very expressive," she mumbled, not realizing she was speaking out loud until he laughed.

"That's probably true." His face was even more open, his eyes crinkled at the corners as his grin took over his face. "My name is Evik, I'm sorry I don't know very many people beyond my own shift. There were just too many people to get to know anyone. What's your name?"

"I am Ariella." Chosen of the gods, she did not include although it was what she would have said to one of her own people.

"So which crew are you on, Ariella? I'm terraforming, not a starwalker," he said.

"Terraforming?" Her tongue struggled with the word she

had no reference for at all. Half of the things Evik said made as much sense as zero current, but she was trying to pick up anything that would tell her what she really needed to know.

"You too? I thought I knew all of us, but I guess in all the commotion to get planet side I didn't get to meet everyone." He ran a hand through his hair and leaned against the trunk of a tree looking up at the night sky and the stars in it.

"I've never wanted more than to get to this place, but I still miss the ship at night." He turned back to her with a soft smile on his face and leaned into her pointing back up at the sky. "Right there, that's our Wheel. I spotted it last night."

She followed his finger to what looked like a tight cluster of stars, they were so closely packed together they looked like a circle shaped star, but that wasn't one she had ever seen before. So whatever his Wheel was, whatever a ship was, it wasn't a star, but it sat among them. Starwalker, that was one of his words.

These people had some kind of star magic. That was the only thing that made any sense.

Ariella looked back to the crackling light as he dropped his hand. Maybe it was part of their star magic, maybe stars looked like that snapping light but far away.

"Hmmm," she said. "Far away."

She looked back up at the stars and forgot to not think out loud until he said, "Yeah."

"But," he said, smiling wide again, "we finally got it working now, right? I mean, look on the bright side, I think we'll be able to start really expanding the land mass in a couple days. Then we'll be able to bring everyone down soon. Not so far away anymore. At least, that's what I keep telling myself."

"Expanding the land mass." Ariella's voice was flat, even to her own ears there was zero vibration to her words, it was just a statement of fact.

A statement of horrifying, world ending fact.

These people wanted to expand the land mass in her world which would fundamentally change the balance of the seas and currents and migratory patterns of the animals int he water. To say nothing of what it would do to her home.

"Where is the expansion?" she asked, her voice shaking and stumbling on the words that made her want to vomit.

"Have you been in the spindle this whole time?" He shook his head, glancing at the massive wall in the center of the clearing. "You must have been. Rough adjusting? Yeah, I heard some people have been with the medics, sorry that was you."

Evik put a hand on her shoulder; a light, tentative touch that lasted for a fraction of a second, but it was long enough to send her heart hammering in her chest and make him wipe his hand on his grey wrap on his legs.

"You should really get a fresh uniform before the humidity collected in that one makes you cold and sick just by being constantly wet. It isn't good for your skin."

"I'm fine." She swallowed and hoped he didn't hear the vibration of panic in her voice that she did.

"Expansion?" She tried again to get him to answer. This was the answer, nothing else mattered. None of the other strange things he said could she allow herself to get distracted by, she had to know this. Above all, this.

"Oh, yeah. Well, the first couple times we tried the terraforming pulses and other ways of stimuli, and the vegetation here didn't respond the way we thought it would." He stood up straight and waved his hand, beckoning her forward as he started to walk.

"Come on, it's actually fascinating the way this planet is set up. I'll show you what we figured out."

Ariella looked back the way she had come through the

bushes, wondering if she should turn around and head back to the arms of the water before the pain took over.

Instead, she balled her hands into fists and walked after him.

Even as he walked up a ramp and into an opening she hadn't seen before in the side of the wall that seemed to go on forever, even then she followed him, clenching her jaw to keep herself moving.

8

Her hand shook, but she reached out and touched the side of the wall as she walked through it anyway. It was hard, slick, and cold. It was not scaled, nor was it like the obsidian her people used for anything that even came close to what the feel of the thing evoked in her mind.

Even by touch, she had no idea what the wall was made out of. But she started to understand that the tall thing was hollow on the inside like rooms.

She followed Evik as he turned and held a finger to his lips in a signal she didn't understand.

They walked through corridors and rooms until they came to a series of what looked like tiny walls stacked on top of each other.

Ariella watched Evik's feet as he stepped up them like he was climbing over bushes and she followed suit, grasping onto the wall as she went.

"I wish they would get the lift working again. But the engineering guy said he needs to make a part to do that and we won't bring the machines down until one of the other spindles come. But, geez, walking all these stairs sucks."

She didn't argue with the disgust and irritation in his voice as they traversed a vast space filled with things she didn't understand and couldn't guess at what they were.

The next set of stairs was more see through than the last and clanged as they made their way up again.

Above the stairs seemed to be a huge open circle that went up forever into darkness that she wasn't sure was the sky or not. Tracking all the way up the tunnel were the things he called stairs curling around the edges.

What was this place? How many more of his people were inside it? And what in the water did they do with all of the stuff everywhere?

The only way to find an answer to any of her questions was to follow him while the pain in her legs stabbed all the way through her with every step and the feeling of the foreign world around her bled deeper into her.

He brought her to a large circle in the middle of one space, hanging from the ceiling.

Inside her head every different material and thing she had ever seen in her life flashed behind her eyes, their properties and the ways in which she understood what they were and how they functioned and that their function followed their form all went through her mind.

Nothing. Not a thing in the whole of her world gave her any clue or insight into what she was looking at in the spindle.

Evik didn't seem to notice anything amiss with the look on her face, although she was sure she must have looked like she wanted to be anywhere but in that strange room.

"Come here, Ariella. I want to show you what we figured out," he said, waving her to his side.

She moved to where she thought he meant for her to go, but

he cocked his head to the side and furrowed his brow at her so she must have been wrong.

But looking around she couldn't figure out where she actually needed to be.

"That landing sickness must be bad," he said, shaking his head and taking her gently by the arm to maneuver her into position right next to him.

It wasn't dark like outside, but he didn't seem to notice the waving of her veil or the feeling of the water as it sluiced over his hands. Only after he took his hands away did he wipe them on his wrap again.

Ariella bit her lip and tried even harder to refocus her ability, her illusion had to look as real as possible. The last thing she wanted was for him to react to her veil while she was inside whatever this thing was.

She repressed a shudder and he tapped at the air in the middle of the circle.

Images flashed and grew outward toward them.

"Right here is the island and see," he said, tapping so the image twisted around and flipped and she could see clearly the bottom of the intricate foliage where it trailed in the water.

She drowned him out as he explained things she already knew about her own world and the interworking of the floating islands and the water.

Her people had long known the workings of their world and here was this interloper chattering away as if he was teaching her something new and surprising.

It was everything she could do to repress her urge to tell him just to get him to stop. It made her have second hand embarrassment, which pulled her focus away from her gifts long enough that the pain in her legs shot a fresh wave of agony through her.

Focus, she told herself.

"But we finally figured out how to get it to anchor itself to the sea floor and we think we know how to get it to replicate the chemical composition of the sea floor when it hits it. So we'll actually be able to create soil up here on the surface. Isn't that great?" He turned a huge smile to her and she twitched her lips back. It was all she could muster.

"That means the sea floor will grow stalks of itself and the islands will be fixed in place?" It was the longest sentence she had spoken since first revealing herself, and nothing about it was something she wanted to say.

Worse was that he nodded, his smile even bigger.

"Exactly, watch. We did a mock-up of what we think we'll be able to do in a year." He tapped and tugged at the floating image and it turned into an orb that started out covered in blue with tiny rare patches of green. But it morphed like her tail did, turning from mostly blue to half brown. Not even green, it was half brown.

She sucked in a breath and choked, coughing as she stumbled back the way she came.

"Ariella?" he called out after her but stayed where he was, tapping at his horror display.

A flick of her hand behind her cleared the water from his ears, but she didn't stop to make sure.

There was no way she could let these people do that to her world, they would destroy it.

But they had star magic, how was she supposed to stop them by herself? Why would they listen to her? Why would he?

Her ruse to get him to talk seemed like the worst possible choice to her as she ran as fast as her awkward gait would go. She couldn't even reveal herself to him and beg him to go away. He thought she was one of them.

World killers.

9

Crashing through the foliage in the darkness, not bothering to beware the sound or the heed the tripping hazards, she fell onto her hands and knees at the edge of the healthy island and where it turned into the ugly scarred new part of the shore.

A sob wrenched through her and she hauled herself to her feet, running the last few steps to the edge and diving into the perfection of the water.

She let it cover her and hold her as the morph changed her legs back into her pain free tail and her lungs back into ones that could process the water.

The first whole breath she took of the cool wash of the water was ruined by the choking tears that she felt vibrating her sadness into the water around her.

"Miranda," she said, knowing the sea would carry it to her friend, including the broken vibration of her voice.

But there was no hiding what she knew, she had to involve the sanctuary, the witch, and Fantos. This was everyone's problem.

It took mere moments for Miranda to catch up to her as she swam toward home.

"What happened?" Miranda's voice trembled and even without the vibrations through the water Ariella knew her friend was edging close to panic.

Unfortunately, there was little she was going to say to make Miranda feel any better about their situation. In fact, she didn't think panic was unwarranted.

"It's so bad," Ariella said, telling Miranda everything, trying as best she could to explain things she didn't have the proper words for, things she didn't even have the concepts for.

As she spoke, her speed increased and Miranda kept pace with her. She was sure her friend's heart was pounding as hard as hers was as they pushed themselves to speeds they never travelled in, let alone for so long a duration.

Passing through the black, she barely felt the chill, their passage was so swift and their bodies working so hard the cold had no time to register in any deep way. She was beyond something so trivial.

Without saying a word as to her intention, she made the sharp turn toward the sanctuary when they dropped out of the black, Miranda made the same maneuver at the exact same time. She must have known that the only first stop that made sense was the sanctuary, and the witch.

Just beyond the main city limits was the entrance to the sanctuary, the intricate dead coral archways and tubes that created the appearance of a giant sea floor creature lying in wait for whatever person or animal wanted to do it harm.

The malevolent appearance of the entrance wasn't crafted, it wasn't carefully formed, or something anyone even wrote down the origins of. As far as any of them knew, there was no evidence that it didn't come from the gods themselves, as a gift of protection for her people. Nothing and no one was willing to risk coming within the reach of what looked like a fierce and menacing guardian.

Miranda and Ariella slowed up enough to weave their way through the paths leading within the coral that no one but the initiated into the sanctuary knew, relying on the initiated to lead them within if there was ever a need to seek shelter.

For the first time in her life, as she passed through the winding way, Ariella thought they would actually have to do the theoretical hiding of the city within the sanctuary. She was one of the ones tapped to do the escorting, as was Miranda, but she wasn't sure if all of the people charged with that responsibility would actually make the trip again and again and risk themselves in the process. Part of her wasn't even sure if she was brave enough to do it, and she had the gifts to help her.

Making it just past the maze of coral, Ariella and Miranda entered the thin fissure in the sea floor into the thickest of black, even deeper and more absolute than the cold black on the way to the surface. The dead coral of the entrance didn't give off any light to shine down into the crack and all that allowed them to keep swimming down into the void was that they knew what was on the other side and could feel the oppressive weight of the rocks all around them threatening anyone who second guessed and tried to turn around in the tight space.

One second the way ahead was devoid of sound and light; the next it burst into both all around them.

Beyond the fissure the best of their world was found. Millions of fish and animals swam in and amongst the people who lived within the sanctuary and the plants that swayed in the currents created by the passage of so many fish.

The whole yawning cavern was lit by brilliant blue and white coral that painted the underground part of their world in variations of the two colors.

Without saying a word to Miranda, they both increased their speed once their tails got beyond the reach of the rocks.

Diving straight for the corner where the gaping maw of the witch's lair could only be glimpsed beyond the fronds of a massive kelp bed, they went so fast that it disturbed the people and the fish going about their business.

Everyone stopped and stared, or stopped and waited, until they passed by and the water settled behind them to continue on their own missions.

Ariella didn't care much if she disturbed all of their lives, if it kept them all alive, she would do a lot more than disturb if she had to.

She wasn't sure what she had to do, or what would be required of her, but she knew her first and next step.

Nothing under the waves scared her as much as the creature in the depths that they called the witch, but she had never gone faster toward her fear.

Please have an answer, she begged in her mind.

The witch was known for her refusal to answer basic questions, other times she answered in riddles, and still others she was truthful to the point of cruelty.

Even with everything in water at risk, Ariella knew there was no guarantee that the witch would help them. There was no guarantee she would agree to hear them out.

But Ariella was gifted by the gods themselves. It was the witch that had taught her how to use her powers, how to control them and call on them.

In her head, Ariella beseeched the gods: *make the witch help us, please.*

She had asked them for many things over the course of her life, but nothing had ever been more urgent in her vibrations, and she knew that nothing had mattered more than that one request.

The question was, would it be answered.

That was what echoed inside her head as she passed through the kelp bed to stare into wide darkness of the cave of the voice of the gods themselves, the cave of the sea witch.

1 0

THE WHOLE SANCTUARY WAS WARM AND SERENE TO THE POINT OF meditative, but for the sea witch's home.

Being on the threshold of entering the deeper cave always made the kelp fronds at her back feel oppressive as they waved over her head, and the rocks along the edge of the opening seemed more jagged and dangerous. It didn't matter how many times she came to see the witch, swimming into her home was always the worst part.

"Do you want me to go with you?" Miranda asked, fidgeting next to her.

"No." Ariella shook her head and gave her a weak smile. "But if you could tell the rest of the sanctuary so Fantos can be alerted, just tell them exactly what I told you. They need to know about the star magic."

Part of her wanted to call Miranda back as she swam away. Part of her didn't like the idea of her people destroying Evik song with his people. He was kind to her, which Fantos never was, and no one other than Miranda had been before she got her gifts.

Instead of listening to that small part of her, she entered the cave, the weight of the space laying on her the second she passed the entryway and was properly in the dark. It happened the same every time, even though she knew better than to fear, her heart beat faster than it should have.

The weight of the air around her pressed her toward the floor so she was swimming just above the ground, at risk of scraping her tail on the rocks.

"Ariella," the witch's voice called through the water, beyond her actual hearing, but the vibration was as strong as if she was right next to her. "Why are you so upset?"

She knew better than to answer until she was in front of the witch. A person only made the mistake of doing that once. The witch yelling at her was one of the most frightening memories she carried; there was no way she was going to repeat the mistake. The witch was just letting her know how much emotional baggage she was dragging in with her like a bad current.

Through the labyrinthine tunnels Ariella swam ever closer to the witch, and the smell of timeless age. The sanctuary taught that the sea witch wasn't the only one they had ever had. It was a role gifted by the gods when they deemed it necessary to move from one to another, but no one remembered a time that anyone else was the witch. No one even knew the witch's original name.

Once, exactly once, Ariella asked what her name was.

No one knew. And no one was going to find out if the witch had anything to say about it.

Ever further down she swam, her heart beat slowing as she did. No histrionics came into the witch's cavern with one of the gifted.

Miranda didn't have the same reaction. But the sanctuary taught that the gifted responded to the presence of the witch, it was one of the ways they tested the recipients of gifts. To see if they truly were chosen by the gods.

Eventually, she reached the end of the tunnels and entered the witch's home.

While the vent she slept in was pleasantly warm, the witch's cavern was hot and the only place under the water that the light matched Ariella's hair color.

No coral grew down here to light the room, but the rocks themselves glowed in shades of red, some even brighter than the hair that flowed around her shoulders as she waited for the witch to make her entrance.

"So, what is troubling you?" the witch asked, appearing from behind a curtain of netting with bones strung through it.

Of all the colors of the people in the city and the sanctuary, all the many hair and skin tones, the witch was the only one without any color to her at all.

The red light reflected off her white scales so that she almost looked pink, but her skin, eyes, and hair completely devoid of color made it clear that the pink was just an illusion. It didn't matter how often she saw the witch, the difference in her appearance to anyone else always struck Ariella anew when she saw her, this time it was even more pronounced after the browns of the star magic people.

"People, people we've never seen before, have come to one of the islands on the surface." Ariella shook her head, searching for the words to explain all she knew, and what she didn't.

She tried again, telling the witch everything, even the parts she left out of her tale to Miranda, like that she didn't think Evik was bad, but he didn't know how bad his actions would impact her world. She even told the witch about the circle and the stairs, the strange interior of the spindle.

The witch didn't speak for a long while, just stared at Ariella with her face that never gave away her emotions.

Finally, the witch held her hands out at her sides and called the water to push her toward Ariella.

She came a hand's breadth from Ariella's face and placed her palm on her cheek. Scales popped out of the witch's palm, scratching at her face.

Ariella sucked in a breath, her tail shaking, but she held still while she felt the witch travel through her mind to see what she had seen and feel what she had felt.

When she dropped her hand from her face, it was everything Ariella could do to hold herself in place and not swim back into the tunnel the way she came, but she couldn't repress the shudder that ran through her.

"People they may be, but they are not our people at all," the witch said, using the water to move her to a soft sea plant that she curled her tail into.

"No, they are not our people, and what they want to do would kill our people. But how do we stop them when there are more of them and they have star magic?" Ariella swam closer to the witch, hope springing up inside her.

The witch was the wisest and most powerful of them all, surely she would know what to do.

"Yes, they would be very destructive, but I wonder." The witch cocked her blank white head to the side and stared unblinking at Ariella.

"Wonder?" Ariella's voice cracked and she knew her fear made it into her vibration because the witch threw her head back and laughed.

"I wondered, but you just answered me. Come back when you are not afraid to do what must be done." The witch waved a hand in a lazy gesture and Ariella shut her eyes against the force that slammed into her.

Opening her eyes again, Ariella found herself facing the kelp bed outside the witch's cavern.

She screamed, allowing herself the temporary rage that the witch would play her cryptic games even now when there wasn't time.

Fantos and others were probably already on their way to the surface to confront the new people, she had to get there to do the only thing she could think of if the witch wouldn't help.

There was no guarantee she would get there in time, and no guarantee it would work, but she shoved her doubts to the bottom of her tail and used them to propel her even faster as she broke the rules of the sanctuary and rocketed out past everyone, swimming fast enough through the fissure to scratch her arm on a rock and leave a trail of blood in the water behind her.

SHE WAS TOO LATE, SHE THOUGHT AS A BODY, BLOODIED AND broken, floated past her.

The surface was so close, she could see more bodies scattered, and some tails of her own people as they fought from the water.

One of them had to be Fantos. He was more deadly from the water than he ever would have been on the island.

It didn't seem like he had used the war gift yet.

None of the others would have needed to keep fighting if he had. Well, unless the star magic was even more powerful than his war gift. But Ariella shook her head, not wanting to even think about that. If that were true, all would be lost.

She swam faster, bursting through the surface and morphing in the air as she screened onto land. The weight of her body crashing down on her not fully formed legs sent a shockwave through her nerve endings and she shoved her pain out of her palms, hitting a tree that toppled over, a gauge taken out of the trunk.

It was the most damage she had ever done with a force and it left her gulping down as much air as she could get into her surface lungs.

There wasn't time to put a veil on to block the pain, and if she did and she needed to call the full strength of a force again, would it work while part of her power was diverted to a veil?

She wasn't sure, and doubt was enough to make her walk without it, sharp stabs accompanying every step.

It wasn't hard to guess where the star people would be making their stand.

Ariella made her way to the spindle and a cacophony of noise coming from that direction.

Grunts, screams, and the slamming of people and objects against each other met her as she stepped through the line of trees into the clearing.

Bodies littered the ground, the door to the spindle was closed, and Fantos stood over Evik, the great poisonous spine of a caraspear fish held aloft to deliver the killing blow.

Evik's face was battered and one of his arms hung at an awkward angle while he sat among the blood soaked foliage, a gash in his leg, and a sneer on his face.

"No," Ariella screamed, throwing her hands out and shoving every bit of her desperation out of her body.

Fantos had time to turn enough to look at her before he was sent flying off his feet and crashing into the trees beyond.

She ran, her gait awkward and her body making her pay for each movement.

But she made her way across the battlefield to Evik, who sat with his mouth hanging open and his eyes wide.

Fantos pushed his way through the fallen and snapped trees, his face a mask of rage and hatred.

"We need to keep him alive to be questioned by the sea witch," she said. At the word sea witch, Fantos screwed his face up, turning him from a menacing warrior into a petulant and impotent child.

He spat on the ground, bloody spittle dribbling down his chin before he swiped it away.

"Fine. But he's your responsibility, and he's getting locked up every second." Fantos turned his head out to the rest of the clearing and bellowed, "No other survivors! I'll take care of it."

She wanted to argue. She wanted to explain that they needed the spindle intact if they were going to understand enough about their star magic to stop the rest of Evik's people from doing the same thing Evik was about to do.

But Fantos wasn't going to listen, and she knew it. He turned away from the clearing and stomped through the trees.

Ariella waved a hand and water filled Evik's ears, not as clean or as stealthily as it had the night before, it left him rubbing at his ears with his good hand.

"Can you stand?" she asked, not waiting for him to answer before she pulled him to his feet.

"How do you know my language?" he asked, dropping his hand and turning his dumbfounded look on her again.

"I'll explain later; we need to get to the shore. Now." She dragged him along, her legs screaming as she did, and he stumbled and limped beside her, his face twisting in his own pain.

"Where did all these people come from?" he asked, struggling to catch a breath while they climbed though the line of trees.

"Stop talking. You're wasting energy and we need to move faster." She doubled her pace, racing against the hammering of her heart while a mantra of, make it to the water, played over and over again in her head.

Maybe stopping Fantos was a mistake. Maybe invoking the word of the sea witch would prove to be a terrible decision she would come to regret. But maybe it would buy her time to find out the full answers to the question of how to save her world.

Ariella couldn't second guess herself, she had to get them out of the way of the war gift.

Finally, they reached the shore and she didn't wait to morph before she shoved Evik in the water and jumped in behind him, pulling him down deeper while her tail came back and the searing pain in her chest told her she could breathe underwater again.

Evik panicked as they went further down and fought against her hold on him, trying to head back up to the surface.

She put a hand over his face and formed an orb of water that filtered the air out so he had a pocket of air covering his nose and mouth.

He stopped struggling and breathed deeply until his eyes stopped being so wide.

When he finally seemed to have his panic under control, she turned to dive still deeper and he wrenched himself from her grasp waving frantically in front of himself, his eyes back to huge.

She followed his gaze to her own tail and she couldn't help it, she laughed.

"You can't breathe underwater or morph?" She shook her head and then furrowed her brow. "What are you?"

"I'm human. What the hell are you? This planet is supposed to only have animals. What the hell is all of this?" He waved his arms again and she approached him, slow and careful like she would a wounded caraspear fish.

"This is me; my people are normally like this. We only have legs when we need them. And we have lots of animals, but you need to come with me. Right now. We don't have time for this." She took hold of his arm again and steered them toward the deep.

Behind them, the sea reverberated with a massive crash, Ariella turned to see the spindle and the entire surface of the island tilt into the water.

The island flipped all the way over, dumping the spindle, debris, and bodies into the water, it all floated down around them while another blast of force shoved the spindle, which Ariella could see was a long tube that came to a point on one end, far off into the sea.

At least it wasn't going to land on the city, but Evik slumped against her and the light went out in his eyes.

1 2

THE ONLY WAY SHE WAS SURE HE WASN'T DEAD WAS BY HIS continued breathing and his continued heart beats. But he was lifeless all the same.

She wasn't sure if she should risk taking him directly to the sea witch or not. And she knew she couldn't take him anywhere else but the cage they used for dangerous animals when they had to.

"I'm sorry," she whispered as she turned toward the cage and bit her lip.

Part of her was apologizing for the cage, but another part of her was apologizing for the loss of his people.

Yes, his people were trying to destroy hers, but watching it hit him was harder for her to handle than she thought it would be.

He didn't stir as they passed through the dark, but his body shivered until his teeth chattered together.

There was nothing she could do; she didn't have a warming gift. But it gave her an idea of a way to follow Fantos's rule and still be more in charge of the prisoner so she could keep him alive until she brought him to the sea witch.

When she exited the black, she took a detour to the place the cage was kept.

Putting a closed eyed Evik down in a corner, she focused on what she wanted to do, pushing the doubt out of her mind about the scale of the magic she was about to use.

But it worked.

An orb enveloped the cage, lifting it off its dais.

She grabbed Evik and flicked her hand, the orb followed her commands as they left the room and traveled the long way around the city to the back arch of her space where she dropped the cage right on top of her vent.

Evik still didn't react when she placed him inside the cage or even when she shut the door and locked it.

But some time later, he did curl up in the warmth of the vent and fall asleep.

Fantos would check on them eventually, and she didn't want to think about what horrible things he was doing to the spindle and any other survivors among Evik's people. The only positive side to his enjoyment of cruelty was that it would keep him busy for a while.

Maybe it would be long enough for her to ask Evik questions herself.

The first person to find them wasn't Fantos, it was Miranda.

"Of all the stupid risks you've taken, this has to be the biggest," Miranda said, curling up next to Ariella and staring at the cage and Evik within it.

"Well, if you have any suggestions that would be less risky, please, tell me." Ariella turned to look at her friend, knowing that her vibrations were all over the place.

"Does the sea witch know about him?" Miranda waved a hand toward the cage and raised a brow at Ariella.

"Not that he's here, not yet. How do I find the time to tell her? And you didn't hear her, she's not ready to tell me what we need to know." Ariella shook her head and focused back on the man in her vent, and what the witch could have meant.

"I hate it when she does that, did she speak in a riddle, or just tell you not yet?" Miranda's vibration held more fear than anger, but Ariella couldn't argue with the sentiment.

"Worse. She laughed and told me I wasn't ready. But I hope she will be able to tell me more after a couple days when I bring him to her. If. If I bring him to her." She swallowed, hard.

"Fantos." Miranda's vibration was thick with the trepidation in Ariella's heart.

The likelihood of Fantos allowing Evik time to heal and the witch time to decide to tell Ariella what she needed to know, was plankton sized.

"At least the sanctuary isn't about to contradict you since you said the witch asked you to do it. Although, I doubt the witch asked you to house him here." Miranda shook her head again and laughed without humor.

"Stop, okay? Where else was I supposed to put him? Besides, he's hurt and he was shivering. The vent was the only thing I could think to do to keep him warm and I have no idea what to do about his injuries." She bit her lip and moved closer to the cage to get a better look at him while he slept.

"You could…" Miranda trailed off and Ariella turned to watch while Miranda bit her lip and swam in circles for a while before she finished.

When Miranda was ready, she squared her shoulders and looked at Ariella head on with a fierceness in her eyes that had not been there moments before.

"Could you use your gifts? To heal him, I mean." Her face was fierce, but her vibration said she was scared.

As she should be, Ariella's mouth dropped open. What would happen if she used her gift on this star magic person?

"The gods gave me these gifts for our people, not whatever people he is. They might take them away if I used them on him. It is absolutely not an option." What was Miranda thinking?

"But you used them to save him, right? How is this any different?" Miranda threw her hands in the air.

"I used them on Fantos. Yes, it stopped him from killing Evik, but it was still on Fantos. And Fantos is fair game. I've hit Fantos before in training. That doesn't risk the gods' wrath."

Miranda snorted a half laugh and Ariella whirled on her, her gifts itching at her hands.

"This isn't funny. What if the gods really do take the powers away?"

"So what? You don't even want them. Not really. You don't want to go thought the ritual and you know that's part of the gifts. Why not lose them so someone who does want to do their duty can have a chance to be given the gifts?" Miranda's vibration was like a sneer, snide and small.

Ariella couldn't believe she hadn't seen it before. They were such close friends she thought she knew everything about Miranda, and she told her things she told no one else. But she saw, with sudden and sickening clarity, that what she thought was true of her friend and her friendship with her, was merely a calm sea hiding a deep and swift current.

"You want the gifts for yourself," Ariella said, her voice no louder than a breath.

Miranda reared back, shaking her head and looking around the room as if the gods themselves would come through an archway to strike out at her for her pride.

"No, no. No, it's just that you don't want it and tons of other people do. There are people who even love Fantos because he's gifted they hold the gifts so highly. But you don't. It doesn't make sense for you to have the power you do."

She held still while she watched Miranda fidget and scramble, knowing suddenly and with every part of her why she was given the gifts.

"That's why the gods gave them to me, because I didn't want them," Ariella said, her voice hushed and her vibrations held a unique sadness that rode along with understanding and… peace.

For the first time since she developed her powers, she was at peace with them.

13

"That doesn't make any sense." Miranda dropped her gaze to the floor and Ariella turned her back on her.

If she didn't understand it, Ariella wasn't in charge of helping her get there. She had bigger things to worry about.

She bit her lip as she stared at Evik while he slept.

He shook in his sleep, a shiver that caused the frown lines on his face to deepen and she knew it wasn't because he was cold. With the vent pouring warmth over him every second, she wondered if it was the pain that kept him asleep and shaking.

The door to the cage was easy to unlock and open by sending a small current of water through the mechanism.

"Ariella," Miranda said behind her, her vibration full of warning, as Ariella swam through the doorway and into the vent.

The lower half of Evik's face was still covered in the orb that filtered the water so he had a constant bubble of air. It moved in and out, swirling all the while.

She cocked her head to the side and studied him, trying to

plot a course for what she would be able to do to help him and what, if anything, she was willing to try.

His arm still hung at an angle that she knew wouldn't have been right among her own people. She thought his arms worked like hers did, and if that was the case then his was broken.

The gash on his leg had long ago stopped bleeding, but the flesh directly around the wound looked inflamed and enlarged, like it was growing away from his body.

It was also taking on a grayish cast that matched the wrap he wore.

She reached out a hand and stopped, holding it close to Evik's leg, but not wanting to touch the wound itself. What if these people had poisonous blood? Would she have noticed a disturbance in the water if that were true? She wasn't sure. Of anything.

Ariella took a shuddering breath and touched Evik's leg. He whimpered and tried to pull his legs away, but she waved her other hand, wrapping his leg with water to hold it in place.

Underneath her hand, his leg was hot to the touch and she felt it throbbing.

He tossed and turned as she closed her eyes and gave a gentle shove of her magic, filling it with healing and wholeness. She avoided specifics of what that would look like our what needed to be done inside his body, as she didn't know. Instead, she focused on the idea of what he needed. It was harder to do, especially as she tried to not send too much, just enough.

When she felt the heat from his wound lessen, she pulled her hand back.

The gods didn't stop her, the gods didn't take her powers away, the orb still swirled in front of his face.

But his leg was knitting itself back together as she watched.

"Oh," Miranda said behind her, her vibration only full of awe.

No one had seen her do any healing outside of the sea witch, she wasn't even sure she had done it right. But, it was better than before and she had to trust herself and her power.

Clearly, she was the only one who did.

His arm was going to be harder for her to fix. She wasn't sure she could fix it since it was deep inside tissue she couldn't even name let alone picture. Did he have different bones than she did? There was no way to know.

"Does he have other injuries? Why don't you wake him up and ask him about them so you can help better?" Miranda asked.

But Ariella shook her head.

Not only was he still asleep, which she thought must have meant he needed to be, but how would he explain his own tissue structure to her in a way that made sense? It wasn't like he could compare the differences, because he didn't know if there were any.

There was only one thing she could think to do and her heart picked up speed in her chest while the hairs on the back of her neck stood on end just thinking about it.

If the gods had left her powers intact before, her plan still might make them snatch them away.

She leaned down toward Evik's face, scrunched in pain, behind his orb of air.

Breaking her own face through the edge of the orb felt like the water was dancing over her skin, like it was welcoming her to the air on the other side.

Of course she couldn't breathe in while she was on the air side so she had to act fast.

She pulled her power into her heart and pushed it through her lungs into the orb and beyond as he took it within himself.

Continuing to push, she focused on health and wholeness

from the inside out. Not on a specific thing again, but on what the general goal was.

Pouring all the magic out of her and into the orb left her body screaming for a breath, but still she kept going, pushing herself to the limit of her ability. If this didn't work all her troubles may have been for naught. And that was the last thing she wanted to happen.

Finally, she couldn't hold off breathing any more, and she pulled back from his face, reforming the orb with a wave of her hand before it collapsed in on him.

She slumped to the side, dragging in ragged and shuddering breaths, even her tail lay lifeless in the flow of the vent.

Evik's face slowly cleared of the lines, the frown, and the crease between his brows.

Then he opened his eyes.

14

His eyes took a minute to focus, when he did he sat up and scrambled through the water away from her, ungainly and awkward.

"You're welcome," she wheezed and he pulled his head even further back from her as he clutched at the bars of the cage behind him.

"Where am I? What is this?" he asked, clutching at the orb in front of his face.

"Stop it, you idiot," Miranda said from the other side of the vent. "If you take that off your face, you won't be able to breathe."

In her head, Ariella described Miranda's vibration as an eye roll. If she had been capable of it, she might have laughed.

"What is happening?" he asked, the fight was going out of his voice, instead his strange and off vibration was more like he was just confused and maybe scared.

Frustration stabbed through Ariella that she still didn't understand him at all. This human as he called himself.

"You are in my city, in my room, in my vent. And I just healed your wounds." Ariella watched as his eyes came back from the edge of panic and he dropped his head to look down at his chest.

"Do you remember now?" she asked, her voice hushed and when he nodded his head, she backed out of the cage, closing it behind her and slumping to the floor on the safer side of the bars.

"So, what now?" He didn't look up, but dropped his hand from the bars to hang in the water in front of him.

"Now, we wait. I don't know what happens next. It's not like people with star magic show up every day," Ariella said, her voice losing steam and her eyelids starting to close.

"Miranda, I need you to watch out for Fantos or the sanctuary. Wake me," she said, falling fast asleep.

When she woke up, it was to Miranda shaking her arm.

"You need to take him to the sea witch now. The decision was made by a council not to consult the sanctuary or the witch at all. They want to kill him. You have to go. Now," Miranda said, shoving Evik toward her.

"Wait, how did he get out?" Ariella rubbed at her eyes and took hold of his arm, realizing her eyes weren't focusing properly and she still felt depleted.

"I got him out, now go." Miranda shoved them toward the back archway and Ariella didn't stop to ask any more questions, just ran her hand along her friend's arm in a silent thank you, hoping she would have time later to say so much more. Including that she was sorry she thought their friendship changed by the gifts.

Swimming with Evik was more difficult than swimming on her own. He was a cumbersome drag on her already low reserves of energy.

"Alright, this isn't working as well as we need it to. Wrap your arms around my neck like this," she said, wrapping one arm over one of her shoulders and across her chest and the other arm under one her shoulders and across her chest like he was a child riding her back.

Finally, they were making good speed headed toward the sanctuary.

But she slowed when she realized that the fissure was lined with guardians. A quick scan proved to her that Fantos wasn't among them, he must have just sent some of his group there to block her should she show up.

"That doesn't look like it's a good thing for us," Evik said over her shoulder, reminding her that she was in this with him now. They were an us for as long as it took for them to get through this and for her to find out how to stop his people from hurting her world.

"No, it is not a good thing. Now, listen, I need you to close your eyes, wrap your legs around my waist, and hold on no matter what. Got it?" She asked, not waiting for him to answer before she dove away from the fissure but toward the sea floor.

He scrambled to get his legs around her waist, finally locking his ankles together and his grip on her was fierce.

She couldn't worry about whether he had heeded her warning and closed his eyes too. There wasn't time to check.

Pushing her body beyond its exhaustion, she was a streak that was barely seen as she crossed between two of the guardians and jackknifed into the fissure, the momentum pulling Evik's body away from her back and then slamming him back into her.

She grunted but didn't let it slow her down. Through the fissure at just the point it was the widest and not allowing herself to veer in her trajectory at all she barreled them through the dark space until they exploded into the sanctuary on the other side.

People scattered and flung themselves out of her way as she rocketed past them toward the lair of the sea witch.

Even blowing through the kelp bed, she didn't slow, it was only when she was navigating the narrow tubes and tunnels to the sea witch's cavern that she choked up on her speed at all. But even then she took the trip faster than she ever had on the way in before.

It was a huge risk, but she wanted to get this over with and the longer it took for Fantos to find her, the more likely he was to look for her in the sanctuary.

The last thing she thought she would be able to handle, was a full offensive array of Fantos and the other guardians.

She thought her best option to get Evik's people to back off was to get him back to his other star people. If Fantos and the guardians attacked her, there was zero chance she would be able to make that happen.

But before she could do anything, she needed the sea witch.

"Ariella? Who is that with you?" The sea witch's call though the water reached her right before she, with Evik wrapped tight to her, barged into the sea witch's cavern.

It took everything in her to stop herself from barreling them into the wall on the other side of the opening.

But she did stop them. And Evik let go of her to tumble to the sea floor, his eyes giant, his mouth open, and his chest heaving.

"Didn't," she started, breathing heavily herself as she floated down to curl up next to him, "I tell you to close your eyes."

"How, exactly, do you think you two are going to get past the massive contingent of people collecting at the fissure?" The sea witch asked, floating into view in front of them. "Especially as exhausted as you are."

Ariella wasn't sure if her tired mind was playing tricks on her or not, but she could have sworn the witch shook her head and frowned her unmoving face before she waved a hand and Ariella's eyes closed.

15

<hr>

WHEN SHE WOKE, THE FIRST THING SHE WANTED TO DO WAS
scream at the witch, but she knew better than that so she settled
for screaming inside her mind.

The witch stared at her, curled in her place and Ariella
thought that maybe she heard her internal wails.

If she did, Ariella wasn't that concerned. It served her right
after derailing the best escape plan Ariella had.

"Neither one of us needed to sleep bad enough for you to
force us to get trapped here. We needed to get out before there
were too many. You had to know that," Ariella said, not quite
able to take all the malice out of her vibration.

"They were already there, in greater numbers than when you
snuck past them. It wouldn't have worked."

Evik stirred beside her, but he didn't wake.

She looked from him to the witch and took a deep breath.
She wouldn't win an argument against the witch, and she still
needed her help to get out of the mess she was in.

Ariella rubbed her hands over her face and shoved her anger
to the end of her tail.

"Please, the last time you said I wasn't ready. But I am now. How do I protect the people from the humans?" Ariella asked, gesturing to the sleeping form of Evik beside her.

"You needed your strength. That was why you slept." The witch still wasn't answering her question, just going around in circles like she was stuck on their previous topic.

Talking to her was always a lesson on patience and Ariella was running low. She bit her lip and squeezed her eyes shut, waiting for the witch to focus on what she actually needed from her. Not the nonsense parts of her distraction.

"Fantos and the other guardians need a fight before they take out their wrath on the people. You must be strong enough for the fight."

"I can't fight him. The guardians, maybe some, but not all. But Fantos… how would I fight against the war gift if he used it on me?" she asked, thinking of the overturned island and the toppled spindle.

"Have you ever tried to produce a wave of that size?" the sea witch asked like she was asking what was for dinner.

"Of course not. No one ever gets the war gift. The fact that he did is not just rare, but frightening. Why would I try?" The sea witch knew things about the gifts that no one else did, so even suggesting Ariella could have the war gift made her look closer at the witch.

When the two were chosen, they always had a few gifts in common and some that were unique unto each of them. That was the way it worked. But of all the many gifts they had, there was no way the two of them would be the first chosen in history to both have the war gift.

"You healed the human." The witch said it like a statement; it wasn't a question and the change of topic surprised Ariella.

"I had to. We couldn't go anywhere or have you talk to him about his people if he was dead." Part of her wanted to yell and throw things, this conversation was stupid and not helping at all.

"The healing gift is not something you use often and you just found out the extent of it, you can heal something not even of this world. You also have the ability to throw a force, and what is the war gift, but a very strong force." The witch waved a hand and the water in front of her gathered and frothed in such a way that it looked like the island with the spindle still on it. Then she pushed with her other hand A massive wave, twice as tall as the spindle and three times as deep as the trailing roots of the island, washed across the scene, destroying everything.

"Are…" Ariella trailed off and coughed, before trying again. "Are you saying that you want me to use the war gift against the guardians and Fantos?"

Of all the things she thought the witch was going to say, of all the ways she thought the witch might help her through the gauntlet of threats outside the fissure, it wasn't by suggesting she attempt to kill the entire collection of guardians and Fantos.

"Would Fantos use the war gift against you?" The witch didn't move, even though her words made the whole sea feel like it shifted places while Ariella watched.

"Yes." Ariella's voice was low and rough. "Yes, I think he would."

The witch didn't react to that, she didn't even flinch. She was as unmoved and seemingly devoid of caring about the outcome of the fight as the glowing rocks around her.

Ariella had to get her answers to all her questions. If she was going to use the war gift on her own people, or even think about it, she needed to know there was a reason. That if she used it and the worst tragedy happened, that she killed people, she needed to know she would be able to save her world.

"How do I stop the humans? They can destroy everything. How do I make them stop? Shouldn't we ask him? Shouldn't you?" Ariella asked, so close to breaking down and begging the witch to do something, to actually help. For once.

"First, you must survive this. Only then will it matter enough for you to find out. Only then will you be ready to do what you must. Just know, there is little reason for the guardians to be. There has not been war for too long to remember." The witch drifted toward where Ariella was curled on the floor and gestured for her to get up.

She swam up to meet the witch and waited for more information that could upend her thoughts, the dread was building to be almost visible in the red light of the cavern.

"Why do the guardians exist?" the witch whispered, not even her mouth moved as she spoke the words.

"Because… I mean, in case of war. Like right now," Ariella said, bunching her brow together trying to puzzle out where the witch was going with this.

"There is no war. Even now. There are the gifts. There is the sanctuary and the witch. There is no need for guardians, so why do they exist?" The witch's pearlescent scales seemed to refract more of the red light than normal; it made Ariella blink and want to look away.

"Fantos doubled the number of guardians and kicked out a bunch of people from their ranks when he got his gifts." Ariella wasn't answering because she still didn't know how, but she was running through every single thing she knew about them in her head.

"And do Fantos and his guardians guard anyone when there aren't humans coming in from the stars?" The witch asked, floating even closer to Ariella so she loomed in from of her, blocking her view of anything else.

"No. No they don't." Ariella closed her hands into fists and swam out of the tunnels, leaving behind the witch and Evik.

16

———

SHE EXITED THE WITCH'S CAVERN AT A STEADY, BUT NOT breakneck pace, relishing in the power she felt coursing through her.

It wasn't the forced nap that fueled her. It wasn't the witch's words even. It was anger. It was rage.

Fantos and the guardians had turned the once quiet presence of their order into an ugly contingent of bullies who did nothing to better their city or their world as a whole.

The last time she tried to bring something to their attention that they should have cared about and done something about, they laughed instead of heeding her words. That laughter carried her through the sanctuary, blinding her to the emptiness of the place.

People were always moving about in the sanctuary, but not as Ariella passed through it on her way to confront the people that should have been on her side and protecting the population.

Heading into the dark of the fissure Ariella made a decision. As much as she wanted to surprise them and lash out right away, bursting through the fissure, she thought she owed it to the people waiting on the other side to give them a chance to leave the area.

Maybe some of them would agree with her. Maybe. She tried not to think it was a long shot to avoid confrontation, but she didn't want to hurt any of her people, no matter how angry she was. It just wasn't in the realm of possibility in her mind to deliberately hurt anyone. She wasn't Fantos.

His influence was toxic. She knew that. But the speed at which it had overtaken people who she would have said were decent and caring, still shocked her. Maybe she missed things in their personalities and they weren't as good as she had thought them once to be. Maybe they were always small, petty bullies more than willing to lash out over any imagined slight and they only cared for themselves all along. But if any of them were wishing every day, as she did, that Fantos wasn't gifted, then she had to give those people a chance.

Maybe she was too proud, maybe she took too much stock in the fact that she must be able to use the war gift if the witch mentioned it, but it was the best chance she had. And she was just mad enough to do it.

But first, she slowed as neared the end of the fissure. She couldn't see out to the other side, but the vibrations of a lot of people talking made their way to her.

There really were more people out there than there had been when she came to the sanctuary.

"I want to go into the sanctuary," Fantos said from somewhere around the edge of the fissure.

"No. That would break every rule, destroy any shot you have of the people listening to you. The sanctuary and the witch are still more important than you are. You can't bring a fight in there." The words weren't audible to Ariella, they were vibrations so strong it was like someone was screaming right next to her.

Whoever the person was, they weren't wrong. And maybe, just maybe they were one of the ones that would head away from the fissure.

She took a deep breath and filled an orb with her command, her request, and her warning. She poured her vibrations into the words so that they hit everyone exactly as she needed them to. If the people who wanted to have a way out didn't leave, it wasn't because she had done something halfway.

It wasn't magic she used to fill the orb with her vibration, it was just the love of her people and her greatest wish that they be able to go back to their lives away from this. That they not have their world destroyed by star magic, or by each other.

The orb rose, up and out through the fissure. The second people grew aware of it floating in front of them she heard the gasps, the mumbled questions, she felt the fear as their vibrations washed over her.

A flick of her hand burst the orb and her own voice poured out to all the people on the other side.

"I am one of the two. The two gifted by the gods to serve the people. The two chosen to be what their people need when they need them.

It is true that I never wanted to be gifted. Not like Fantos, who wanted it for his own power and influence. No, I didn't want the responsibility of all of your lives weighing on mine.

But I will not argue with the gods themselves. They gave me this responsibility, and I take it as a sacred duty. The gods didn't give me my gifts so I could throw a half thought temper tantrum like Fantos did and make it so we couldn't stop the humans from destroying our world with their star magic.

Now, we have one last chance to stop the star magic. That is why I took the human to the witch. So she will instruct me.

What I need in order to do what must be done, is for all of you to go back to the city.

Everything in our world could be destroyed if you do not. And if you do not, if you choose to stay and try to obstruct me in my given mission from the gods, as I'm sure Fantos will instruct you to, I will have no choice but to fight you all.

I do not wish to hurt my own people, but I will if you insist on trying to stop me from saving them."

The noise outside the fissure grew too loud for Ariella to make out single voices, or what anyone was saying. But she felt their vibrations, so much of which was fear.

Voices diminished, many were leaving, she felt their decisions, their acceptance and determination on her behalf. But not everyone left.

"Come out here, Ariella. We are not afraid of your little forces." Fantos didn't need to use an orb. His voice was a boom that carried to her without any diminishing of his exact words.

Fine, she thought.

He wanted a fight, but there was no way he was prepared for what she was about to do.

She shut her eyes and tried to pinpoint where his vibration was coming from, where he was outside the fissure.

In her mind she pictured the chasm, the waiting guardians, Fantos floating in the center, directly over the dark maw of the fissure.

Her fingers curled her hands into fists so tight her knuckles ached.

But she used it.

The pain, the heartache over her people, the fear for her world, and the rage.

Oh, the rage.

She turned all of it into fuel for a force, but one bigger than she had ever created before. A wave so large, so instantaneous, that no one would be able to hold it off, so complete that the people on the other side of the fissure would be left limping their way back to the city and not able to bother her again.

Focusing on it became the whole of her world, every single bit of her essence and her magic poured into her singular need.

A wave crashed in the sea beyond the fissure. She heard it form and crash into the people on the other side like the entire city had collapsed at once. The reverberation of the impact knocked her back from her place in the dark.

She swam out of the fissure right behind the tail end of the war gift passing overhead.

No one stood around the opening, but there was a large crowd collected on the edge of the city far in the distance.

In the opposite direction of the city she watched as a mountain of water, almost a solid thing in its weight and size, rolled through the sea showing no sign of slowing yet.

Part of her wanted to go check on the people who would be tossed aside by the force of her wave when it finally began to wane. Instead she held her head high, the power in her not diminished by her achievement, but strengthened by it. It tingled down her back and to the tip of her tail.

She turned and headed back into the fissure, to finally get the instructions she needed from the witch.

It was time.

17

Entering the witch's cavern with her entire body still bussing from her magic, she saw for the first time that there were no echoes inside of other people. Most places that people inhabited for a lifetime still held the echoes of their presence long after they were gone.

Like the names of previous people were written on the walls and every now and then you noticed it when you were looking right at it.

But the witch's cavern was different.

There was no echo, there wasn't even a hint. It was as if the cavern only existed for the witch to live in and did not exist prior to her being there it was so imprinted with her essence.

Ariella missed the moment the witch revealed herself she was so immersed in looking around d and noticing the way the cavern felt different after her use of the war gift.

"Well done. It seems you may now be ready," the witch said and Ariella snapped her attention to where the witch floated just beyond the reach of a still sleeping Evik.

"How old are you?" Ariella's voice came out like a breath she didn't mean to exhale, but the witch's eyes opened wide and her mouth turned into a feral snarl with her teeth bared.

"You dare?" the witch hissed.

Maybe she should have apologized, but Ariella couldn't think about the word sorry, she was stuck in the age of the creature before her.

She had a wild image pop into her mind that the witch was one of the gods and she was more than ancient. She was primary. That without the witch, her world would not exist.

"You." Ariella couldn't say more, and she thought the witch understood what her monosyllable meant because her face fell back to the flat one devoid of emotion. Like the witch was only capable of mimicking real emotion for short periods of time.

It sent a wave of tingles through her scales.

"There is limited time before his people are going to send reinforcements. You must do what needs to be done before they make their move." The witch waved a finger and the water pushed Ariella toward Evik.

"What must I do?" Ariella still had not been given anything approximating a real plan and it was starting to make her angry enough to hurt her head.

"Humans have their star magic; we have our own version of the same. You will use it to get you both to his ship and once you are there you will do whatever needs to be done to stop them." The witch waved a hand and Evik floated over to Ariella.

"Use this when you get to the surface." The witch handed her a shell that felt like it was as big as the sea itself it held so much magic.

"Okay," Ariella said, and swallowed. "Thank you."

She meant to say more, because there was so very much to say, but her throat closed up and she just nodded.

The witch nodded back to her and it sent her heart hammering within her chest.

For some reason she couldn't name and didn't understand it felt like she was saying goodbye. But the witch was such an integral part of her world and such a constant presence, especially now that she suspected the witch was as old as the world itself, any thought of saying goodbye to her didn't make any sense.

Ariella shook her head and took hold of Evik, turning and dragging him along with her to begin the long swim to the surface.

Parting the kelp bed before her, she was met with the people of the sanctuary lined up like a processional to a ritual. But this wasn't the ritual she had been dreading that she was headed toward.

It took her a second while her nerves jangled from the response of the sanctuary. They didn't try and waylay her though. They didn't try to stop her from continuing, they were just silent sentinels, watching her as she passed.

The darkness of the fissure was truly welcome as she entered it. No matter how she held her own going between the lines of the sanctuary people, it was strange and uncomfortable, while in the deep dark of the fissure, she only had to worry about continuing to move and not letting Evik get snagged on the rocks.

On the other side of the fissure she was expecting open water and a clear line of sight to the deep she had to pass through to get to the surface.

Instead, the entire rim of the fissure was filled with the people of her city. They had their heads bowed and did not lift them as she swam. Even Miranda, her blue hair almost glowing among the orange green haired people she happened to be near, didn't lift her gaze to meet Ariella's eyes.

They remained bowed as she ascended. Scanning the crowd told her that Fantos and the other guardians were not among the throng.

Her war gift couldn't have carried them so far that they wouldn't have been able to get back if they were well. She did truly hope that they survived.

But for her, for that moment of doing what she had to for the people, only the people bore witness, and it boosted her will to continue.

Whatever the shell, heavy in her hand, did when she activated it on the surface, she was ready. The people were behind her, the sanctuary was behind her, and the witch had set her on this path. She wouldn't look back.

18

Evik started shivering again when they reached the deep, so she expanded his orb to encompass his entire body, blowing air, heated by her own magic, into the orb to mingle with the air it filtered from the water around it.

For all the humans had the magic of the stars, magic she couldn't fathom, they seemed very susceptible to cold. Evik wasn't injured anymore, so it wasn't just that.

She tried to file that new information away with what little she knew of them. None of the puzzle pieces made a lot of sense to her. These beings that had magic enough to travel among the stars, but not enough to keep themselves from injury or cold, were still a mystery for the most part.

The spell that the witch cast on Evik to keep him asleep wouldn't last forever, but Ariella hoped it would last long enough for her to get him to the surface.

An awake Evik, floating in an orb as he thrashed and tried to swim or something, wouldn't help her at all.

It was better if he stayed buoyant and asleep. They were making good time as all she had to do was swim and flick her hand to keep the orb heading in the direction she wanted it to go.

Finally, they were nearing the surface and Evik started to stir.

"Shhh," she said, realizing as she did that he no longer had the water in his ears to allow him to understand her language.

"What the hell? What is this?" he asked, pushing against the orb which swirled around his hand, almost shattering and sending the magic scattering into the water.

Ariella swore under her breath and flicked a hand so water collected deep in his ears again.

"Please stop trying to shatter the orb; if it breaks, you don't have air and I'll have to expend more magic to keep you alive." she wanted to smack him. After all she had done to save him and get to his ship to save her people, he was risking his life to poke at the orb.

"Magic," he said, his face going slack and his hands dropping to his sides.

"Yes, obviously. You have your star magic and I have the gifts of the gods. Although the way you talked about it, your gods must be very powerful if they gave so many people magic." She flicked her hand and the orb zoomed ahead of her for a few minutes until she caught up to it.

His face was scrunched up and looked troubled. She would have asked him what was wrong, but his vibrations were so strange she wasn't sure she would be able to tell for certain that he was telling her the truth.

"But a lot of your people attacked us, are they gifted but he gods too?" His brow was furrowed and his mouth turned down in a frown. It made her think of the dead bodies of his people that floated among the wreckage of the island.

"Everyone can morph, that's just in our bodies, but only Fantos and I are chosen by the gods. When there are chosen, they are only two." She waved her hand again, keeping the orb with her this time.

"Fantos," he said, and she didn't need to feel his vibration to know he knew who she was talking about, and he hated him.

"It is very possible he is dead." She tried to keep her vibration neutral, tried to keep the complicated emotions she felt over killing one of her own, no matter that it was Fantos, from her voice.

"Dead? Very possible? What does that mean?" He looked around him at the water, squinting into the depths like he was going to spot Fantos heading their way.

"It means that I sent the war gift at him, but I didn't try to recover his body." She clenched her hands into fists and waved again to keep the orb floating along beside her. She wanted him to stop talking.

"War gift," he whispered, letting his mouth hang open as he stared at her, his face softening as he did.

There were things she thought about saying to him and his awe, things she discarded one by one as they passed through her mind. Instead, she kept her own council, biting her lip as she continued to keep the orb moving.

All she really wanted was for him to help her speak to his people so she could protect hers. If he did that, all she had done to get him to this point, and get them to his people, would have been worth it. Even the war gift, and the deaths. Even that.

He kept his eyes on her, his mouth a grim line, but he said little and barely moved as they continued their ascent and neared the surface.

"Do you know where your ship is in relation to the island you were on?" she asked, wondering how far she would have to swim them to get closer to it.

"It was directly above it, tracking along with it, turning with the planet to make it easier to stay in fast communication.

They're probably trying to figure out how to get another spindle down here to look for survivors, but the other islands weren't big enough to land on."

Some of what he said still remained impenetrable to her for all the words were translated, their meaning in his world couldn't possibly match their meaning in her world. She still didn't know what a spindle was exactly, other than it was the big thing in the clearing she went into with him.

"What is the spindle made out of? I've never touched something like it. It was like rock or obsidian, but different." She couldn't help but try and at least get that little curiosity guppy answered.

"Metal. It's made of metal. I thought your nets were made of wired metal too," he said, pulling his head back and blinking like he was surprised by her question.

"No. Our nets are made of fin wires from some of the fish, well, I mean the nets used by the guardians against you were made out of fin wires." His face blanched and she bit her lip again.

"Right. Those things suck," he said, turning his head to look out into the water with a pained look on his face.

He wasn't wrong. She got hit with one on accident once and ti felt like it was going to take off her arm. But she couldn't bring herself to apologize to him. Not when his plan had been to destroy her home.

"Where are we going now? What are you planning to do with me?" He asked, his voice hushed and sad even though it was clearly resigned. It was one of the clearest vibrations she had ever received from him.

"The witch gave me a way to take you back to your people. So that's what we do next." She looked to the surface, as they broke through to the air beyond the water.

19

EVIK WAS STILL TRAPPED IN THE ORB, BOBBING ON THE SURFACE OF the water. She waved a hand and it disintegrated gently around him, leaving him free. He chose to use the opportunity to float on his back and look at the stars, breathing deeply.

She looked up at the stars along with him, morphing her lungs to take in the air and allowing herself a deep breath before she used the shell.

"Which one is yours? Can I see it from here?" she asked, not turning away from the shining lights in the dark sea of the night sky.

He bumped up next to her and pointed it out to her.

It didn't matter how many times she told herself that going up there and negotiating directly with the people was the best option, it still put a lump in her throat that was hard to swallow around.

"Okay, are you ready?" she asked; he paddled away and nodded, his face solemn.

"Now, I have to warn you. I don't know what this does. So if I turn into a metal spindle, just brace yourself." She held the shell in her open palm above the water. It was still heavier than made sense for its diminutive size, but the power in it came off like waves.

Taking one last breath, she closed her eyes and focused on opening and activating the powers held dormant within the curves of the shell.

What had been shallow waves, even mere ripples, grew larger and came closer together until it was a constant barrage of power flowing from the shell and into her. She squeezed her eyes even more tightly shut and turned her face to the side as it buffeted against her.

Light exploded on the other side of her eyelids, making her see pink and yellow through her skin. Her hand started to burn but she held still, afraid to drop the shell in the water and lose focus and contact.

But it only burned for a few seconds before the shell lifted itself from her palm. The light grew even stronger, flashing in an array of colors so bright her eyelids barely blocked them from her eyes.

She maintained her focus and her calm, breathing deeply of air that started to taste of heat and storms, of ice and silence. Disparate things that flashed through her mind as the air touched her tongue.

Under the waves her tail started to split, the pain of morphing lessened somehow by the magic. The water pushed her body up and out of it until she dripped in the air as her legs finished forming and a pain like morphing started in her back from between her shoulder blades down to where her back curved inward.

It felt like hot water was pouring over her back in two lines as she arched and flung out her arms trying to find a way away from the pain.

Over years she had grown used to her morphing pain in her

tail, but she had never experienced it in her back and there was no escaping from it. It left her distorting and twisting her body in an attempt to try that she couldn't stop.

Finally, the pain ebbed and the light pulsed slowly away to nothing.

Taking deep breaths, relieved to be doing so without the agony in her back, she opened her eyes to the same night sky and the same open water like nothing had happened.

But then she looked down.

Ariella was high above the water, the last of the sea dripping from her toes, her tail was replaced by legs and out of the corner of her eye she spotted wings made of water and bone that jutted out of her back and moved without her needing to know how to make them move.

"You're going to fly me to my ship? How will we breathe? There is no air in space," Evik said, reminding her shocked mind that he was there, with his eyes wide, chewing on the inside of his cheek.

"Well," she said, flicking her hand and encasing him in another orb that rose from the sea to float beside her.

He swallowed, hard, and she had to suppress a laugh.

If she was being honest, the idea of flying into space was terrifying, but she had to keep a hold on herself if she was going to be able to have the nerve to do it, and laughing at Evik's warranted fear of the situation would only make her feel more out of control.

She flicked her hand again and gave herself a veil of water over her entire body with an air pocket near her nose and mouth.

Part of her wanted to just breathe her water like she was meant to, water that tasted like home and everything she had ever known, but she wasn't sure if she could while she was under the witch's spell.

Instead she simply relished in the feeling of the veil slipping over her, and closed her eyes for a silent, 'I will miss you' to the sea itself.

With nothing left to do but get on with it, she did, flicking her hand to keep the orb holding Evik traveling along with her as she flew higher into the air, getting further and further from her underwater home with every beat of her wings made from it.

Had the gods expected any of this when they granted her the gifts? She wasn't sure she thought they had, but hopefully they were with her while she did what they expected her to do with her powers, whatever she had to.

As they went through the air, high above the sea, she saw that her world was round and the water of her veil, her wings, and the orb all moved faster and she had to keep her hand moving to make sure it didn't just blob up and float away. Whatever natural forces kept water wanting to stay together and helped with her magic, weren't there for her among the stars.

The circle of lights she headed toward grew more and more into focus.

It was actually a giant circle shaped thing that looked a lot like the spindle, grey and metal, rotating around a center with a stack of spindles on it. The lights came form squares that as they drew closer she could see were full of people. Humans.

More of the grey wraps, and more of the various shades of brown hair, made her think that all of Evik's people must have been similar, which was much less diversity than she saw among her own people. She missed the bright colors of her world already and a longing to get home as fast as possible made her pick up her pace despite her body's desire to slow down and rest.

"Just so you know, before we get there, some people might freak out. They've never seen someone," he said, pausing to look at her from the top of her head to her toes, lingering on her wings, "Like you. And, it would be easier if you were wearing something."

"Wearing something?" She understood the word in reference to a wrap, but she was already wearing her wrap. Looking down at herself she wondered if it had fallen off in all the activity and she hadn't noticed. But no, there it was across her chest and around her shoulders, lightweight and soft since it was dry.

"Yes. Um, you see, we wear fabric on our lower half as well. Like my uniform," he said, gesturing at himself and the ugly gray full body wrap.

She wrinkled her nose, but looking at the people in the ship who would be welcoming them, she nodded her head. It was probably better to be respectful of their customs since she was trying to get them to do something she wanted.

A small flick of her hand and the veil around her changed to grey from her neck to her ankles.

"Okay," he said, and shook his head before squinting his eyes at the ship looming before them. "Right there, see that indentation in the side there? That's the airlock entrance."

Following his hand and trying to see what he was pointing at made her want to just magic her way inside somehow. She didn't know what, if any, of her gifts would help her in that regard, but it didn't stop the wish from running through her mind.

Eventually she spotted what she thought he meant was the way in, pointing to it herself as he nodded and she turned them to head toward where she would intersect with the ship's rotation.

"Why is it turning?" she asked, when they finally reached the door and she grabbed onto a handle next to it, using her magic to keep him orb in place along with her. She was well and truly running out of energy.

"The rotation simulates gravity, the force that holds someone down on the ground on the planet. But you need to push that panel there and a door will open. Once we're inside we have to cycle through a couple more doors before you let me out of this bubble." His smile grew and he was leaning forward in the orb like he could barely wait to be out of his confinement.

It struck her as strange, as the door opened at her touch, that he would so readily want to trade one captivity for another. He was a captive in a bubble out here too. It was a turning metal bubble, but still the same idea. Meanwhile, she was the opposite of excited to enter his world.

She stepped inside, her feet and legs not yet aching at the pressure, and brought the orb with Evik in it with her. Behind them the doorway closed and a chill went through her at the thought of being closed within the ship. It was too late to turn back, but it took everything in her not to try to do just that.

Turning back to the way further into the ship, she made the same move when a new doorway opened, stepping through and bringing the orb with her. It made for a tight fit between her wings and the orb, but being in the enclosed space didn't last long before a light changed next to the door and it opened on a small room with strange, empty looking mock ups of humans hung on the walls and a group of people were crowded around, staring and open mouthed.

"Let me out," Evik said, and she wasted no time before she waved her hand and freed him of the orb, bringing the water to herself and merging it with her veil, darkening the colored area of it and uncovering her head.

Her first breath of the ship tasted like hot rock or even magma from an underwater volcano.

Before her, Evik and his people were greeting each other with awe and tears, but strangely no embraces among them. Only one woman put her hand on his shoulder.

In her world, if someone had been away and thought dead, the first people to greet them, no matter their personal relationship with the person, would have at least hugged them.

Not these humans, they kept themselves at an awkward distance from Evik and each other.

"Everyone, this is Ariella. She is gifted among her people and used her gifts to save me and bring me here." Evik held his hand out toward her while every set of eyes in the group focused on her, some of them wide, some of them narrowed and pinched.

She stepped forward, her feet starting to sting, moving her wings so they avoided hitting against the walls or the doorway.

A young person with the same short hair as Evik except theirs was black and they had deep brown skin, barreled around the corner, people in the crowd jumping out of the way as the person flung themselves into Evik's arms and kissed him full on the mouth as Evik clutched the person to him in a an almost fevered way.

Now that was something her people didn't do. It was interesting to see them kiss so deeply and with so much passion. The only kisses she had ever seen were short and a sign of respect, not this clear show of romantic love.

Of course, she could have been wrong. Ariella had never been interested in romance or love. It was part of why giving herself to Fantos in the ritual was the last thing she wanted to do. Not only was she not interested in the idea of it, but to have to do so with Fantos who the last person she would have chosen? No. Just thinking about it made her stomach flop over.

Finally, Evik and his companion pulled apart, keeping a tight hold on each other. For all the distance the others in the group of humans kept, they didn't blink at the display of affection before them.

"Temple, Ariella saved me," Evik said, gesturing to her and Temple next to him beamed with tears in their eyes. "Ariella, this is my husband, Temple."

She dipped her head in acknowledgement and Temple must have taken that as a sign to approach her, although it wasn't what she meant.

He crossed the distance between them and took her hands in his, tears were still swimming in his eyes.

"In a million universes I never would have thought I would say thank you from the bottom of my heart to a woman with wings, but here we are. You brought him back to me, if there is anything I can do for you, please just ask." Temple smiled at her and her heart picked up its pace.

"Anything? Well, then please take your ship away from my world," she said and offered a smile in return.

Temple's smile faltered and he looked back at Evik while keeping a hold of her hands.

"Do you know what she said?" He asked.

"Oh, I'm sorry," she said, waving a hand and filling all the ears around her with water from her veil so she wouldn't have the same problem.

"Ah," one person said, rubbing their ear, while a few others tried to shake the water loose.

"Now you should all be able to understand me," Ariella said and everyone but Evik's mouth dropped open, some even took a step back or held a hand out like they could stop her from saying anything else.

"Temple, it is nice to meet you. What I request is that your ship leave my world alone and do not return there. Your terraforming magic will destroy my world. And I can't let that happen." She tried for another smile, but Temple seemed frozen in place before her.

"Well, um, Ariella we don't make that decision. The leadership team would make that decision," Evik said, stepping closer to her and putting his hand around Temple's waist.

"Please bring me to the leadership team, Evik," she said, letting go of Temple's hands and taking a step forward.

"Is your uniform moving?" One of the collected people was staring down at her stomach and the greyness of her veil.

"Yes. It's water. Most of my magic is water based for obvious reasons; our gods are water gods, after all." Ariella wanted to say something about the person's rudeness, but she bit her lip. These people didn't know anything about her, she had to remember that. Besides, she was there for a reason. Arguing with someone who couldn't help her wasn't working toward her goal.

"Why is her water magic based?" Temple whispered to Evik as they led the way through the group and down a curving hallway with views occasionally out to the stars.

"The whole planet is water. Even the islands are floating," Evik said, his voice also low.

She wasn't sure why they tried to be quiet, she could hear them with no problem.

"Her legs are temporary, normally she has a tail, and the wings are new. There is… a lot I have to tell you," Evik said, lifting one of Temple's hands to his mouth to kiss his knuckles.

Of all the strangeness of the day, kissing knuckles made Ariella miss a step which sent a sharp stab up her leg. It was just a strange gesture. A knuckle wasn't a cheek or a lip which were the only places she knew of to kiss a person.

"Where is the leadership team? I would like to speak with them right away." She didn't bother to say anything else. She was starting to wilt from being so tired and her legs were already becoming painful.

"I'm sorry, Ariella, but you won't be able to speak with them yet. I need to write a report and they will see you tomorrow, so for now I'm just going to take you to our quarters so you can sleep. It's the best I can do," Evik said, his quiet vibration really did seem apologetic though, so she nodded after a beat of just allowing herself to be disappointed.

Maybe it was better that she got to rest and rejuvenate before she tried to negotiate with the leadership of the star magic humans. But that was assuming she would be able to make her mind shut off enough to sleep, of that she was less than certain.

2 1

"So, um, I don't know how you sleep normally, but this is a bed like what I sleep in," Evik said, gesturing to what looked to Ariella to be a flat rock.

Her legs ached and she longed for the comfort of a warm vent, but this wasn't her world. She bit her lip and tried to figure out what would happen if she lost focus because her exhaustion made her fall asleep instead of just resting.

Would she wake to a puddle of water, her wings gone with no other way to get home? Would she wake to a puddle and no veil to blunt her pain? Would she morph back to her tail?

Never, not one time that she knew of had anyone ever fallen asleep while morphed. She always got back in the water long before sleep was a problem. But the one time she lost focus and dropped out of morph when it wasn't her choice was when she was hit but the human force and that was miserable. There had to be some way to not do that again.

"Is there a place where I can be in water?" she asked, turning to look back at Evik, who eyed her wings more like he was worried she was going to smack something with them than with the awe of the other humans who saw her.

"Um, I don't know where…" He looked to Temple and raised his eyebrows at him.

"Maybe one of the ponds in the terrarium?" Temple said, offering her a shy smile.

"Alright, that's our best option. Come on, Ariella, it's this way."

She followed Evik and Temple down another curved corridor while the people they encountered jumped out of the way and hugged the walls if they didn't dart through a door.

"They're scared, I think," Temple whispered, leaning into Evik's ear.

Humans were scared of her? She watched closely when they passed the next few people in the hallway as they avoided her gaze and squeezed themselves as close to the wall as possible as she passed.

Interesting. Maybe it was a good thing they were frightened.

Perhaps she could use that to her advantage when she met with the leadership.

Finally, they reached a place that was some kind of pretend world different from the rest of the ship. It looked like some of the plants from one of her islands, and plants she had never seen before, were crowding the biggest room she had been in yet.

Taking a deep breath that blessedly tasted clean and almost devoid of hot rocks, she closed her eyes to relish it for a minute, stopping in her tracks.

"Are you okay?" Temple's voice broke into her moment of peace and she snapped her eyes open while trying to suppress the urge to pull the water out of her ears so she didn't have to understand anyone for a while.

"Fine, but I only see plants, not water," she said.

"Oh, right over here," Evik said, gesturing around a bend in the path between trees.

A pond, almost the size of the room Evik had first shown her with the bed in it, sat in the middle of a copse of trees, some of their branches hanging in the water.

She didn't listen to a word Evik or Temple said as she climbed into the pond, the water slowing down some of the pain shooting through her legs.

Without thinking about it, she allowed her veil to drop and focused on holding onto just her wings while her legs morphed back into a tail and she sank into the shallow pool.

Having a tail again almost felt like going home. Almost.

"Tail, she has a tail to go with the wings, okay then," Temple said behind her and for once she didn't mind the intrusion to her thoughts.

She turned around and smiled at him which, for some reason that didn't make a lot of sense to her, made him snap his mouth closed and swallow, hard.

"I will not be sleeping, but I will rest. Do you think it will be safe for me to do so here?" she asked, trying to pick up on their vibrations as they looked at each other and had some kind of silent conversation that hurt her brain to try and puzzle out.

"Just in case, although I think you'll be fine without us, we will rest and wait on the other side of the trees if that would make you more comfortable." Evik gave her a weary smile and he and Temple, their arms around each other's shoulders, moved out of her sight.

Ariella didn't have the same faith in Evik's people that he did, but she hoped that her saving his life would garner some sense of protectiveness from him and Temple.

Still, there was no way she was going to sleep, they didn't

need to know it was in large part a way to preserve her wings. They didn't need to know her magic was limited. Their's wasn't.

A little longer, that was all she needed, just a little longer. Rest, recharge, and reclaim her home as a place for her people alone. Just a little longer.

2 2

WAKING UP IN THE SMALL POOL SHE HAD A MOMENT WHERE SHE
forgot where she was, when it crashed back into her brain with
all the force of a war gift, she spun and splashed desperately
hoping to find her wings had stayed with her.

But falling into her exhaustion, and allowing sleep to over-
take her as she waited for the humans to figure out how to talk
to her, came with a heavy price.

Her wings were gone, the only thing showing in the reflec-
tion on the water were shriveled bones hanging from the places
in her back where her wings should have been.

She closed her eyes, clenched her shaking hands into fists
and took a wavering breath, focusing everything in her on
forming the wings again.

Tingles crossed her back and water collected around the
shriveled and discolored bones, but wings they were not.

Ariella hung her head and tears escaped her eyes. How
would she get home? She couldn't stay in the stars, in a small
pool that wasn't even the right kind of water, without the right
fish to eat, forever.

If she did, she thought forever might be short.

But she didn't have time or space to breakdown and worry. She had to pretend to still have all the powers she did before. There was no way she was going to walk into negotiations with the literal weight of her world on the fragile and useless bones hanging from her back without the safety of them assuming she was in full ownership of her power.

She took a few breaths and sunk beneath the waterline, allowing it to wash away the tears on her face.

The bones in her back stung as cracking and popping filled the water from where they were pulling themselves back into her body, becoming something else entirely in the process.

Writhing in the pool, every few seconds some new part of her body would be exposed to the air and a chill would go through her, setting off the shivers and the pain again. It rolled and flared only to ebb finally, leaving her gasping at the air above the water. Breathing in the ship's strange water was more difficult than it was to breathe at home. It made her lungs angry and her throat want to cough. So she held her breath until she could gasp in the air above the pond's surface.

Her back, and her sides wrapping around her chest, were agony.

Maybe the witch had helped her, but the kindness of the process left a lot to be desired.

Now what was she going to do? How was she going to get home?

She breathed, deep inhales and exhales, holding her world in her mind and forcing herself to focus on saving it first, worrying about herself, about being trapped, after.

First, though, she realized as she looked down at her tail, she was going to have to morph. Again.

Closing her eyes and making the decision to morph, to let go of the last physical hold she had on who she really was, was easier said than done. But eventually, it worked. The pain was almost a welcome reprieve from the agony in her mind. Almost. It was still not what she wanted to have to do and she would be happy if she got back home and was never asked to morph again.

Her legs, sitting in the pool, the look of them distorted by the water if she turned off the part of her vision that automatically filtered the changes, were bare as the rest of her was.

Part of her wanted to not do the veil, not cover herself up for these people when it didn't matter to her in slightest, but she had to use every trick to get them to see her as person enough to listen to.

So she stood on her shaky legs full of angry and screaming nerves, and called the overly full water of the pool, at least some of which was really hers, back to her.

It climbed up her body, enveloping it, calming it, soothing the painful and weary parts. Something inside her, a part she couldn't name or even figure out where it was located, let go of something that allowed her to be relieved she was at least covered in water.

Of course, just being covered in water wasn't enough for the humans. She rolled her eyes as she turned the water to be more opaque and more grey.

"Good morning," Temple said, crashing through the trees and bringing her fully, undeniably back to the reality of the next thing she was going to have to do.

"When do I meet with your leadership?" she asked, lifting her chin and stepping from the pool, appreciating the small amount of pain involved.

"Right to the point." Evik shook his head, but of course she got to the point. She didn't want to be there any longer than she absolutely had to be, it wasn't exactly fun.

"Don't worry, Ariella. We'll take you over there. I'm sure

they're anxious to meet you too." Temple looked from Ariella to Evik and back again with his brow furrowed and a smack to Evik's hand.

Anxious wasn't the word she would have used, but maybe he wasn't wrong. They walked back through the best space on the ship, past pools and trees and plants, and back into the harsh world of their star magic while she tried to think of a way to use that to her advantage.

23

LEADERSHIP, IT TURNED OUT, WAS A COLLECTION OF PEOPLE WHO looked like they should have been allowed to rest and relax into their old age while the weight of decision making fell to the younger people on board. But these people did the opposite of what her people did.

It threw her for a moment as she walked into the cavernous room full of people who stared at her with everything from awe to hatred clear on their faces.

She may not have been able to understand their vibrations as well as her own people, but their faces were so much more expressive than she was used to. With this many of them gathered together, it was overwhelming to watch as their feelings flitted across their faces.

With a flick of her hand, she tried to fill all the ears in the room with water, but it only worked on half of them.

Ariella licked her lips and held her hand palm up, trying the air, feeling out the water within it. There wasn't enough.

People with their ears already full, rubbed at them, one man put his finger in and wriggled it so hard she thought it must have hurt.

There was no way around it, she used some of the water from her veil to fill up the rest of the ears in the room. Everyone needed to hear her, to understand her. Even if it meant that her veil became a touch thinner, a bit more see through, and allowed more pain to get through.

"Everyone, I would like to introduce Ariella," Evik said, holding a hand out toward her.

She stepped forward and held her head high, her face as impassive as she could make it as she studied these leaders who made choices that led to destruction.

"Please sit. We have never met someone who isn't human before." A man with thick grey hair that shown in the lights of the room as if he had the stars themselves woven into his head and skin a deep rich brown color, gestured toward a pillowed place on the floor.

"And I have never met humans before yours came to my home and tried to kill it," she said, pursing her lips as the faces around her changed to something more like anger.

"Now, that is the point, isn't it?" A woman asked, although Ariella wasn't sure which one of a group of three had said it.

"Yes, that is the point of me coming here. You see, your remaking the world, to make the islands larger and connected to the sea floor, would damage my home beyond repair and likely kill many of the species we rely on." If that woman wanted her to be sorry for pointing out the terrible crimes the humans were committing against her people, she was going to be disappointed. She would try for manipulation of their loyalty to Evik, sure, but they had to understand just how dire the situation was.

"But your people attacked ours and Evik was the only one to survive the massacre." The woman again. This time Ariella found who the voice belonged to. She was almost as pale as the witch, but she had light brown in her hair.

"The only reason Evik survived was because I saved him. I killed my own people in order to do so. I want to negotiate so we can stop the killing. Your people's force did damage to me just being hit by it once on the surface. What would it have done in the time it took to grow the islands?" Ariella cocked her head to the side and enjoyed watching the woman shrink before her.

"What is a force?" the man asked and Evik used the word she hated and could barely pronounce, terraforming.

"So it damaged you?" the woman asked, her eyes fevered as she leaned forward.

"Not more so than our force can damage you," Ariella said, her voice acid to her own ears and not sorry about it.

"Please trust me when I say, you don't want that force aimed at you," Evik said with a shudder.

The woman relented, leaning back, but she stared out of the corner of her eyes at Ariella as she did.

"I'm sorry, but the only way we can colonize the planet is to do some from of terraforming. Your islands are just too small for us to even land our spindles on, let alone develop cities." The man said, his face putting the lie to his apology even if she didn't understand some of his other words, she understood a false apology just fine. What did colonize mean?

"You are not sorry, and I think we should be honest with each other if we are to have any good faith conversation here," Ariella said and some of the people actually hung their heads or nodded.

Good, it was a start. But she needed to get a lot more people on board with her in order for this to be successful. She took a deep breath and squared her shoulders to keep going.

"Well, maybe I just don't understand how we can be expected to move on to another planet without even restocking on supplies. We need to stay, and how do we do that if we can't terraform? There has to be a way for both of our people to live on the planet together." The man shook his head and his voice grew in volume as he spoke.

"Because it isn't your planet. It is ours, whatever designs you had on it are irrelevant. Did you really not know that we were there?" she asked, wanting to hit him with a force and instead allowing her voice to fill with vibrations instead. The kind that left her own people cowering before her, but it only worked on a few of the humans.

"I…" The man looked around the room, avoiding eyes contact with everyone, but his one syllable non-answer was all Ariella needed. It told her everything she needed to know.

"Of course we didn't know. I don't know how you fooled our sensors to hide your body heat and the scans never picked up any large mammals at all or any civilization at all." The woman threw her hands in the air, and it was clear she, at least, had not known.

"They live below a layer of extremely cold water; their whole city is below that on the sea floor on heat vents. I think that's why we didn't pick them up," Evik said.

"You may not have picked us up on your scans, but he knew we were there," Ariella said, gesturing to the man with the guilt dripping through his vibration.

"Stanley?" Evik asked, his mouth dropping open.

"Oh, so now you just believe whatever this creature says?" Stanley asked and Ariella clenched her fists.

"Creature is what we call the plankton. I am not a plankton. And unlike you, my words don't smell of guilt and I have lied to no one. What did you know?" Ariella's vibration may not have been full of lies like his, but hers was heavy with barely contained rage she was sure she wasn't the only one to hear.

"I… Nothing. I was aware of nothing about a complex society." The man looked around himself, but he must have seen what she did; the people did not believe him.

"None of that matters. We're here now, and we can't move on to another planet right away. She needs to be able to colonize. That is the bottom line," the woman said while the man nodded along, and Ariella leaned forward, her fists clenched.

"Excuse me?" Ariella asked, her voice was like ice and the hairs on the back of her neck stood on end.

"Whatever you want us to do, there is only one option for us. We must colonize. We have so much of our technology to share with you. You will be better off because of us." The man nodded his head, like he was agreeing with himself.

Ariella curled her lip and wanted to slap the man. Instead, she lifted a hand and shoved a force at the door across the room.

24

<hr>

It slammed out of the frame and crashed against the wall of the hallway. The people sitting around jumped in place and stared at the crumpled mass that used to be the door. A few of them were shaking and it allowed her a moment to breathe deeply of air that tasted of their fear instead of her rage.

"Your technology, which I assume is the name of your terrible star magic that destroys nature, has no place on my world. And we are fine without it." She wanted to shove his star magic back into the stars, deep into the darkness of space where it belonged. But she had to show these people her magic wasn't nothing.

"This conversation," the man started, his voice shaking, "is over. You are a savage and we will not be derailing our whole system to humor you."

"Wait a minute," Evik yelled, holding his hands out in front of himself.

Some of the people seated around the room grumbled, but clearly this person held some kind of power and most were not going to speak out against him.

"No, Evik. I know you have some misplaced sense of loyalty to this alien, but you are seeing her human looking face and ignoring all the rest, the wings, the tail. No. I'm sorry that you went through what you did, but this charade is over. Guards," the man called over his shoulder, waving forward two people who stood against the far wall.

Ariella may not have understood the complicated power dynamics in the room, but she knew the kinds of people headed directly towards her. They may as well have been named Fantos. She also knew the man was wrong. She wasn't an alien. This was her planet.

The guards stomped toward her and she flicked a hand, growing tired of watching their scowls. They flipped upside down and hurtled through the air to crash against the wall and crumple to the ground.

"Go ahead, use your magic against me. It's the only way you're going to stop me from destroying anything, and I mean anything, you send against me." She stood up from the floor, the pain shooting up her legs only further fueling her wrath.

"St… Star magic?" the woman stammered.

Even though it wasn't going to help her in the respect arena, she wanted to roll her eyes at the woman. Fine, if they were going to pretend not to understand her, she would use their clumsy words that made her tongue feel too thick for her mouth.

"Whatever violent technology you have, use it. Hit me. You have no problem with killing my people and the animals on my planet, you have no problem with trying to destroy my civilization, so try it first with me. Kill me." Her back was as straight as it had ever been, she would not cower to these people and their cruelty.

"Monster, that was my son," the man yelled and flung himself at her, his teeth bared.

She flicked her hand and he joined his son, crumpled on the floor in a heap.

"If you choose to pretend I am some kind of lowly creature, if you choose not to care about my people and their well being, then why should I care about your people? I saved one of yours, against one of my own and at great risk to myself. And this is how you repay that act. With disdain and threat to my very world." She stepped between to others, heading toward the door. Even though she didn't have a plan on where to go on the ship, or how she was going to get herself back to her world, she had to get out of that room.

"No, Ariella," Evik called behind her, his voice joined by the shouts of some of the others against him.

"Stop it, Evik. She's a monster with a pretty outside. There is no saving these people. We need to destroy them all. We can't risk it," the woman said, not bothering to be too quiet in the bedlam of voices.

But Ariella heard her.

Turning to look at the woman, whose pale face tinged green under her gaze, Ariella flicked a hand, removing the water from everyone's ears, including her own. She had heard enough.

She could still hear their words and cries as she slammed people around the room, but she didn't understand any of it, and that suited her fine. They needed to be stopped. These people who didn't bother to see others as people. If that responsibility fell to her, so be it.

A particularly stupid one came up behind her—they must have entered from the hallway through the missing door—and slammed into her back, clamping a hand over her mouth like that was going to accomplish anything.

She flicked her hand and took a deep breath, free of their restricting her, without bothering to check to see what happened to them.

Evik grabbed Temple by the hand and they darted from the room.

There was no point in following. They weren't going to hurt her; she didn't think they had it in them. And she would rather not track them down and feel guilt and sadness at killing them if she could help it. The others in the room held none of the same conflicting emotions for her.

Flick, another one dead. Flick, two more.

Piles were starting to form along the walls and still the people in the room kept attacking. The floor she stood on shook rumbled with her power and the impacts of the dead. They kept leaping at her and screaming, their faces reddened and veins pulsing at their throats. It didn't matter what tricks they tried to use against her, she just moved a hand and they were done.

When the last of the leadership was a pummeled mess, she turned to look into the hallway, through the window into space she spotted what looked like another spindle take off toward the deep stars.

Good, some of the people on board must have understood that her world was not theirs. They had better look for another one.

Stepping into the hallway, she realized that people were charging her from both sides, covered by some kind of gear that looked like flat rocks over their faces and their torsos.

Whatever the point of what they wore, it didn't help as they hurtled through the air and slammed against the people behind them.

It did nothing for the one who went sailing through a window, or the ones sucked out after him.

She flicked a hand and the water of her veil, far too thin now, covered her face and the rest of her body, protecting her from the ravages of space that she watched happen to the people she sent into it.

Along the corridor, in doorways leading to the section she was in, as well as just beyond where her attackers had stood, massive metal plates slammed into place. They all looked like the same kind of doorway she and Evik had entered the ship through.

The humans must assume she couldn't get to them on the other side of the metal. Which was true, how was she going to use her magic to stop this threat if she couldn't see them?

But the same part of her that she relied on when she attempted to use the war gift screamed within her as it grew in strength. She felt her body shifting reserves of power and energy to the force within her placed there but he gods.

It didn't matter how far she was from home, the gods were still with her, she could feel them.

Under no circumstances was she going to let her world die. She knew that heading up to the ship. It was the risk she took, but she had hoped to return, she didn't think the gods would ask it of her, what she knew she needed to do.

She thought the gods were going to find a way to save their chosen, to save the gifts.

But they had not saved Fantos. They had not even punished her for hitting him with the war gift.

The part inside of her that she thought was most connected to the gods themselves told her that it was time. What the witch said, about her not being ready, that it was no longer true.

Her breaths were ragged and hitched with sobs as she placed her hands on the wall leading to other rooms and other humans.

"Please just let the part of me inside go home," she said to the powers within her.

Force ripped out of her hands. The strength of it surpassing even what she sent at Fantos. Along with the power, she released an unending scream.

Words couldn't do justice to the feeling coursing through her, a soul deep, guttural scream that sounded like it was tearing apart her vocal chords as the ship ripped itself into shreds around her and the water of her veil dissipated along with physical parts of her own body.

Until the only thing left was water vapor, falling toward the planet, and a people saved by the one chosen of the gods, whose name they would never forget.

AFTERWORD

Thank you for reading! Don't forget to check out the other books by the author at
jdarleneeverly.com

ACKNOWLEDGMENTS

A whole hearted thank you to Bean, the Rottens, and all of my friends and family. A big bag of thanks to Jupiter Alley and Magnolia editing for their help in making this happen, as well as the team at Wishing Well. This was not the story I set out to write when I had the idea for the book, but the characters decided they knew better. They're usually right.